"Put your arms around me?" Cate asked.

"You know where this could lead," Jude said into her hair. "You're far too beautiful for me to resist."

"I want to forget everything for a little while."

"Is that the only reason?" He turned her to look at him.

"Sex can be very liberating." There was more than a hint of bravado in her tone.

"I asked if that was the only reason."

Her expression changed. "You know it isn't."

Margaret Way takes great pleasure in her work and works hard at her pleasure. She enjoys tearing off to the beach with her family at weekends, loves haunting galleries and auctions and is completely given over to French champagne "for every possible joyous occasion." She was born and educated in the river city of Brisbane, Australia, and now lives within sight and sound of beautiful Moreton Bay.

Books by Margaret Way

HARLEQUIN ROMANCE®
3715—MISTAKEN MISTRESS
3727—OUTBACK ANGEL
3767—RUNAWAY WIFE*
3771—OUTBACK BRIDEGROOM*
3775—OUTBACK SURRENDER*

HARLEQUIN SUPERROMANCE®
762—THE AUSTRALIAN HEIRESS
966—THE CATTLE BARON
1039—SECRETS OF THE OUTBACK
1111—SARAH'S BABY*
1183—HOME TO EDEN *

*Koomera Crossing

MARGARET WAY
Innocent Mistress

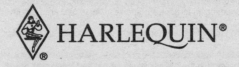

HARLEQUIN®

TORONTO • NEW YORK • LONDON
AMSTERDAM • PARIS • SYDNEY • HAMBURG
STOCKHOLM • ATHENS • TOKYO • MILAN • MADRID
PRAGUE • WARSAW • BUDAPEST • AUCKLAND

ISBN 0-373-03803-8

INNOCENT MISTRESS

First North American Publication 2004.

www.eHarlequin.com

Printed in U.S.A.

CHAPTER ONE

AFTER the well-heeled, well-endowed Poppy Gooding left his office in a swirl of silken perfume, Jude carefully wiped any lingering trace of lipstick from his mouth, then straightened his tie.

"Play it cool, Jude," he advised himself.

It didn't help. He knew he'd had about as many of Poppy's come-ons as he could comfortably deal with. He'd never met a girl so oversexed. He suddenly recalled a movie about sexual harassment in the workplace in which the man was the victim. Poppy's behaviour wasn't as dastardly as that woman's had been but her methods of seduction were at the very least questionable. Poppy completely lacked the degree of reserve one saw in properly brought up young ladies—although maybe that thought belonged in the Dark Ages... She most certainly wasn't a virgin, but then virginity wasn't as valuable as it used to be, either. The key point was that Jude had to stop her before she removed her clothes. Or his. He was the guy who'd always considered mixing business and pleasure high risk. In this instance it could see him right out of a high paid job.

After months of trying to fend her off he'd come to the conclusion Poppy had big plans for him. He was even tempted to get it over with and prove a big disappointment. Two of the guys in the firm, fellow associates, had given service beyond the call of duty. Maybe it was a required course of action? At present he was the guy holding out, resulting in a lot of ribbing from his colleagues.

The big problem was that it would be a bad, bad move

to offend her. Her father just happened to be his boss, Leonard Gooding, senior partner in the prestigious firm of Gooding, Carter and Legge, corporate lawyers. Being invited into this firm usually didn't happen for years, if ever, but he'd earned a lot of kudos along the way. He'd graduated top of his law class with first class honours. He was a good athlete, track and field which didn't hurt, either—even couch potatoes like Leonard Gooding were sports mad. He could only be thankful Poppy had spent the previous six months overseas, no doubt spending a goodly portion of her father's money. It was Poppy, the collector, who'd made the running almost from the day she laid eyes on him.

Women smiled on Jude. He'd be a fool not to have noticed, though it took them a little time to realize how keen he was on his bachelor status. He was twenty-eight years old. There was a lot of exasperating talk about his "blue, blue eyes" among the girls in the office. Blue eyes apparently scored well. The articled clerk, Vanessa, had even told him she wanted to pass his blue eyes on to her children. Even so Vanessa didn't put him on the defensive like Poppy.

City life had enforced his entrenched view of women. Every last one of them was after a husband—preferably a rich one—they'd been brought up that way. It was intimidating for guys. Some of them thought Jude, as a husband, would do nicely.

The only thing was, he wasn't in the running. Not yet. Most guys were happy to start considering marriage when they got to thirty or so but he wasn't sure he would. Not that he played unobtainable—he'd had lots of nice girlfriends—but there were huge problems after The Knot had been tied. Marriage after the marvellous heady flush of the Big Day was a big letdown. Women seemed to live for the day alone as if they were no ever-after to occupy their time. The fabulous wedding dress—it needed to be white, the veil, the masses and masses of flowers, the picturesque church, the reception, just family and friends that turned into a crowd of four hundred. In his opinion, and on the evidence, they'd been planning it since they changed booties for shoes. The trouble was the excitement didn't last and lots of times neither did the attraction.

Statistics proved too many marriages didn't work out. Some of his clients had been married two and three times and they sure as hell didn't give the appearance of being happy. In fact most of them had a henpecked look. Jude didn't want his marriage—if he ever stopped flinching away from the hazards—to be a dismal failure. He didn't want to see another kid, like himself, suffer. If the saddest thing in the world was a mother losing her child, it was just as sad to be a child losing its mother.

These days he got by playing fancy-free man-about-town. A month ago he'd made it into a list of the Ten Sexiest Men in the city, though he'd never returned the call of the woman journalist who had started the whole nonsense. In any event she turned up a glossy photo of him at a function and used that under the heading Local Heartthrob. There was no point in being outraged. Vanessa had made a bumper sticker of it and somehow managed to fix it to the back of his car. All the beeps and the cheeky little waves finally aroused his suspicions and he had stopped in a loading zone and ripped it off. No one seemed to take it seriously anyway, so he'd shrugged off the ribbing. It was a crazy world. Sometimes it didn't seem worthwhile a quiet, country boy like himself trying to hold the line.

Nevertheless he'd changed a lot since his university days. Now he had to dress in sharp suits, shirts and ties, even his socks had been labelled cool by that journalist. He could kill her. Cool socks? That was a brain wave. His unruly blond hair—always had too much curl in it—was cut just right according to Bobbi his secretary who from the beginning had taken pity on him and told him the in places to shop, even where to have his hair cut. He no longer had short back and sides and as a result it skimmed his collar. He couldn't stop it flicking up all over the place. He'd long ceased trying. The guy at the unisex salon who'd cut it told Jude with a roll of his eyes he was a dead ringer for some famous actor. For an eye-popping minute there Jude had thought the man with the scissors was going to kiss him, but no, he settled for a friendly squeeze on the shoulder.

The fact was he'd taken years to get himself together. He'd always liked to be comfortable, even sloppy. T-shirt, jeans, sneakers. He liked going to the gym, working out, as he was still an athlete at heart—he'd even won a bridge-to-city run. For public display he'd had to change in a hurry; he had to look like what he was, a young lawyer on the fast track, cited to get to the top. At the beginning he hadn't minded Poppy's advances all that much—he was as open to temptation as the next guy—if only she could have kept it low-key.

He'd never expected it would please Leonard Gooding who had the kind of granite face you wouldn't wish on anyone—what if it came out in Poppy's children?—if Jude became involved in a meaningful relationship with his only child. The possibilities for Leonard Gooding's future son-in-law were limitless. Hints were already being thrown around about a full partnership by thirty, access to the top clients. There would be fresh territory to roam, an introduction to the charmed world of the hyperrich. Jude would have to laugh at all their jokes and let them beat him at golf.

Born and bred in the middle of nowhere, a small North Queensland sugar town, Jude sometimes thought he might be able to get used to that kind of life. He hadn't studied as hard as he had to be a loser. His much loved Dad had been so proud of him. But then he had to confront a formidable truth. He saw no real possibility of ever selling his soul no matter the rewards.

The only way out for him was if Poppy got interested in someone else and the sooner the better. He realised however hard he worked, however smart he was supposed to be, it wasn't beyond Gooding to turn on him at a moment's notice and engineer his dismissal from the firm. Leonard Gooding was a shark.

Jude walked restlessly to the panoramic plate-glass window that overlooked the broad sweep of the River City. At this time of the afternoon the impressive steel and glass commercial towers were turned to columns of gold by the slanting rays of the sun. Any self-respecting shrink could diagnose his deeply ingrained resistance to matrimony as the by-product of his childhood. His mother had abandoned the best and kindest man in the world, his father. She'd abandoned him, her only child. That single event had influenced his entire mode of thinking.

'My gorgeous boy!''

That was the way she'd used to greet him. What a joke! It depressed him to even think about it. She'd never meant it at all. She was only acknowledging that physically he'd taken after her. He'd been a bright kid going on twelve, thinking all was right with his world, when she took off for the beckoning horizons. He only found out years later when his father finally told him the whole pathetic story, that his mother had gone away with a rich American tourist who had been holidaying at the luxury hotel where she was receptionist. His mother in those days was a knock-out. She was probably still able to turn heads with her golden blond hair, big melting blue eyes and luscious figure. According to his all-forgiving father no man could be blamed for falling in love with Jude's mother, Sally. Sally was perfect.

It took Jude years to come to the realisation that when it came to his mother, his father had been one gullible fool. Even as a kid he'd been edgily aware that his mother who the gang he hung around with described as "hot" was a habitual flirt. She gave off allure like a body scent. Probably the rich Texan hadn't been her first affair. At the time his father told him his mother needed a more exciting life. The town was a rural backwater.

"Sally wants a real taste of life. She's so beautiful! She deserves more than I can give her."

Did that excuse being unfaithful? Jude didn't think so. His father had let himself be seen as dull and boring when the fact was he had been a clever, industrious, respected town lawyer. He loved books, revered literature. He loved music, too, classical, jazz, opera and he adored big game fishing. He had such a great sense of humour. Much as Jude's father had grieved, extraordinarily he'd never held a grudge against his wife.

Jude did. Unlike his father he'd never wished his mother all the best. He and his father had been betrayed and Jude had learned the lesson that women weren't to be trusted. They cheated on their husbands. If they didn't get what they wanted, they moved on. If his father continued to love his mother until the day he died, Jude took the opposite stand. He might be thought hard and judgmental, but he hated her for sucking all the life out of his father who died soon after Jude made it into the firm. His father had flown to Brisbane so they could have a celebratory dinner together. He'd been so proud, telling Jude before he left, his dearest wish was that Jude would have a much better life than he had.

"Find the right girl. Marry her. Give me grandchildren. You're the one who always kept me going, Jude. I've lived for you, son. You've done me proud."

Trying to make his father proud was what had given him

the edge, driven him to succeed. Then his father up and died
on him. At least he'd been doing what he loved—big game
fishing. He and a couple of his life-long pals were out on
Calypso when a freak electrical storm hit. The waves, re-
portedly, had been huge. His father and one of his friends
had been washed overboard. Both perished in the Coral Sea.
Despite a wide search their bodies had never been found.

How I miss him! Jude thought, grief locked deep inside
him. The town had given him all the sympathy in the world
when he flew home for the memorial service. He and his
dad had always been popular. He was the local boy made
good. Now that he had a real chance of making it up to his
dad for all his sacrifices his dad wasn't around. Successful
as he'd become the loss of his father shadowed Jude's life.
There's no end to love in the human heart; no end to grief
when love is lost.

Bobbi, Jude's secretary tapped lightly on his door, breaking up his melancholy reflections.

"Manage to get rid of her?" Her hazel eyes were full of
wry humour. Bobbi was petite, attractive, power dressed and
happily engaged. Since he'd been with the firm she'd proved
a real friend and a great legal secretary, loyal, thorough and
accurate. He got on well with her sports reporter fiancé,
Bryan as well.

"Don't look so damned happy," Jude groaned. "It was
really, really hard." He moved back to his desk. "Poppy
Gooding has deluded herself into thinking she fancies me."

"And how!" Bobbi choked on a laugh. "I nearly had
cardiac arrest when she shoved past me. She mightn't look
like Leonard—she must get down on her knees every night
and thank the Lord for it—but she's a bulldozer just like
him. She only wants you for your body, friend."

"Why the heck me?" he asked in extreme irritation.

He really means it, Bobbi thought. Jude Conroy, every

girl's dream! A drop-dead gorgeous hunk with those dreamy, dreamy blue eyes! He even had a fan club in the building. If she and Bryan weren't destined for each other Bobbi thought she'd have thrown her own cap in the ring.

"Want me to put around the rumour you're gay?" she asked drolly.

He shot her a sharp glance that softened into his white lopsided grin. It made even the faithful Bobbi's heart execute a little dance. If he wanted to, Jude could star in a toothpaste commercial.

"I doubt that would stop Poppy. She'd think she was the one girl who could turn a man around. What I need right now is a vacation."

His cell phone rang when he was walking to his car later that afternoon. It was Bobbi on the line, her voice flustered.

"Listen, I just had a guy on the phone, kind of snarly sort of guy I bet kicks his dog, severely put out you weren't here—name of Ralph Rogan. Says you know him. Wants to speak to you ASAP. Sounded like you were sleeping with his wife. I told him you were due for an important meeting that should break up around four. Number is—your part of the world curiously—got a pen?"

"Give it to me, I'll remember."

She laughed. "Jude, you're a human calculator."

"Right." He had a special thing with numbers. Even as a kid he'd been able to add up stacks of them in his head not that kids used those skills anymore. Bobbi gave it to him and from the area code he immediately identified his area of Far Northern Queensland. He didn't need any introduction to Ralph. Ralph Rogan was the son of the richest man in his home town of Isis and one of the richest men in the tropical north. Jude's dad had been Lester Rogan's solicitor and close confidant. Rogan Senior had trusted no one except Jude's father. Jude and Ralph had gone to school together but they had never been friends. More like adversaries. The hostility was an on-going state of affairs exacerbated by Ralph's "problems" with his domineering father. Rogan Senior had wanted and expected his son to shine, to come out on top. Ralph never had. Even as a boy he'd been to use Bobbi's word, "snarly," a bully who traded on the fact his father practically owned the town and huge tracts of land for development. It had to be something serious for Ralph to get on the phone to Jude. As soon as the meeting was over he'd place a call.

Piercing screams woke him, screams that echoed around the mansion. The minute Ralph Rogan heard his mother's frenzied cries, he knew something was very wrong. It had to be his father. His father had been diagnosed with atherosclerosis, hardening of the arteries. It wasn't surprising after a lifetime of indulgence, eating, drinking, smoking, womanising. Despite the warnings it never occurred to him to give anything up. With any luck he was dead. Ralph had lost every skerrick of affection for that big bull of a man who was his father. He didn't consider he closely resembled his father at the same age.

Ralph shot out of bed, pulling on jeans and a shirt in a great hurry. He didn't bother finding shoes. He rushed into the hallway, covering the not inconsiderable distance to his father's suite in the west wing in record time. His mother and father hadn't shared a bedroom in years. In his arrogance and insensitivity—Lester Rogan thought of his wife and children as property—he'd brought in workman to turn several rooms of the family mansion into a self-contained suite for himself. Ralph's long-suffering mother had no back bone. She was a thin pitiful thing these days and she'd been left out in the cold. His father was like that: a law unto himself. That's what came of too much money and power.

Inside the massive bedroom with its heavy Victorian furniture inappropriate to the climate Ralph found his mother slumped to the floor beside his father's bed. She was sobbing bitterly, her thin body convulsing as though shocked and grieved out of her mind.

"I couldn't sleep. I knew something had happened." She turned her head, choking on her tears. "He's gone, Ralph. He's gone."

"And good riddance." Ralph Rogan let a lifetime of bitterness and resentment rip out. For moments he stood staring at his father's body, his heavy, handsome face dark with brooding, a thick blue vein throbbing in his temple. Eventually he moved to check if his father was indeed dead. A huge man in life, in death Lester Rogan looked surprisingly lighter, shorter, his mouth thrown open and his jaw slack. His eyes were still open, staring sightlessly at the ceiling. Ralph reached down to shut them, but abruptly drew back as if the corpse would rise up and bite him. He didn't want to touch the man who had treated him so badly, who had never shown an ounce of pleasure or pride in him. All he'd received were insults and humiliations, comparisons with that clever bastard, Jude Conroy, the Golden Boy.

"He's dead all right!" Coldly he informed his weeping mother, throwing the sheet over his father's face with something approaching violence. "I'll get Atwell over. He'll have to sign the death certificate." Ralph cast another disgusted look at his mother, before drawing her to her feet. "What the hell are you crying about, Ma?" he demanded in genuine amazement. "He treated you like dirt. He never had a kind word for you. He kicked you out of his bed. He had other women."

"I loved him," his mother said, disengaging herself from

her son's hard grasp and collapsing into one of the huge maroon leather armchairs custom built for her husband. It dwarfed her. "We were happy once."

Ralph's laugh was near wild. "What a load of drivel! It must have been a lifetime ago. There's never been any happiness in this house. You'll have to pull yourself together while I phone Atwell. Where's Jinx?"

"Please don't call your sister that, Ralph," his mother pleaded. "Sometimes you're so cruel."

He rounded on her, tall and burly, deep-set dark eyes, large straight nose, square jaw, already at twenty-eight carrying too much weight. "I didn't give her the nickname, remember? It was Dad. Okay, where's Mel?"

"Here, Ralph." A light soprano voice spoke from the door. "He can't be dead." Melinda Rogan cast one horrified glance at the sheeted figure on the bed, then advanced fearfully into the room.

"He is, darling." Myra Rogan answered, holding out her hand to her dressing gowned daughter. Melinda was two years younger than her brother, a pretty young woman with her mother's small neat features, soft brown hair and grey eyes.

"Well I'll be damned!" Ralph mocked. "He never did a thing the doc told him."

"It's such a shock, Ralph." Melinda swallowed on the hard lump in her throat. Bravely she went to tend to her mother, putting her arms around Myra's thin shoulders. "Don't weep for him, Mum," she said gently, her own eyes bright with unshed tears. Death was death after all. "He never showed you any kindness."

"He did once," Myra insisted, rocking herself back and forth.

"Oh, yeah, when?" Ralph busy pushing buttons on the phone looked towards them to bark.

Myra tried to think when her husband had been kind to her. "Before you were born, a few years after that," she said vaguely. Lester Rogan had taken little notice of his daughter.

"So he never cared for me from day one," Ralph snarled.

"That's not true. He loved you. He had great plans for you." The fact that these plans never worked out was not always Lester's fault.

Abruptly Ralph held up a staying hand, speaking into the phone to his father's doctor.

"Here, Mum," Melinda found a box of tissues. Copious tears were streaming down her mother's face, dampening the front of her nightgown. Once her mother had been pretty, but for years now she had been neglecting herself, horribly aware her husband had no use for her.

"Atwell will be here in twenty minutes," Ralph informed them. "Could you please stop all that hypocritical blubbing, Mum, and get yourself dressed. That man in the bed there—" he jerked a thumb over his shoulder "—has done us a huge favour. At long last we're free of him and his cruel tongue."

"Surely you mean at long last you can get your hands on the money," Melinda challenged, suddenly looking at her brother as though he were the enemy. "You're head of the family now. I tell you what, Ralph, I'll take a bet you'll turn out no better than Dad."

It was hours before Ralph Rogan was able to make his phone call to his old sparring partner, Jude Conroy. Good old Jude, the big success story. The hotshot lawyer. There was no love lost between them. Once when they were kids, around thirteen, Conroy had whipped him good and proper for bullying some new kid, a snivelling little runt, small as a girl, who'd been admitted to their excellent boys' school on scholarship. Ralph had never forgotten lying on the ground, wiping the blood from his nose and his mouth—a loose tooth. It was easy to beat up other kids. It was humiliating to be beaten up yourself. One day he swore he'd get even with Jude Conroy, school hero, champion of the underdog, young lion. Even Ralph's mother had said he'd probably deserved his beating, taking Conroy's side.

His father and Conroy's father had been real close. Matthew Conroy had been his dad's solicitor. Conroy knew all the secrets and he'd taken them down to the deep with him. Now Ralph was going to need a solicitor and loathe as he was to contact Jude, he knew he had to. Matthew Conroy had drawn up his father's will but in the event of his death Lester Rogan had appointed Jude executor.

Lester Rogan's funeral was underway before a young woman slipped into the back pew of the church. She knelt for a moment, then sat back quietly. A navy silk scarf was wound around her hair in such a way not a tendril escaped. She wore a simple navy shift dress. A few people at the back of the church turned to glance at her. Most were caught up in the eulogies, as first Ralph Rogan, then various townspeople walked to the podium to endeavour to say a few words for the late Lester Rogan, whose real estate kingdom included half the town and stretched for miles.

Though everyone tried—some better than others—there was no real feeling, not even from his son who stood with his hand over his heart, face beaded with sweat in the heat, rambling on about what a giant among men his father had been; how his father had taught him everything he knew. This had caused a little sardonic ripple to pass through the congregation that was quickly brought under control. Lester Rogan had not been loved and admired. Over the years he had become as mean as they come. Collective wisdom suggested Ralph was shaping up to be a chip off the old block.

The family sat up the front, son and daughter with their faces blank, Myra Rogan inexplicably weeping uncontrollably as though her husband had been the finest man ever to walk the earth.

Tears of joy, a lot of the congregation thought waspishly. She'd get over it. Probably take a grand tour overseas. There never had been any evidence Lester Rogan had physically abused his wife or children, but he'd kept tight control on them, allowing his wife and daughter little real freedom. At the same time they had benefited from his money. They lived in a sprawling two-storey mansion atop a hill with the most breath-taking view of the ocean. The womenfolk were able to buy anything they wanted—clothes, cars, things to keep them entertained—though Myra Rogan wasn't anywhere near as attractive as she used to be. The expensive black suit she wore with a black and white printed blouse was much too big for her. The stylish, wide-brimmed hat with a fetching spray of dark grey and white feathers, spoiled by her haggard unmade up face.

Jude, who had arrived a scant ten minutes before the service began sat rows back on the family's side of the aisle. How different this was to the memorial service that had been held for his father. Then the old timber church had been packed with mourners spilling four deep into the grounds. Today it was half filled.

People had wept as they spoke about Matthew Conroy's innumerable kindnesses and the generosity which he'd wanted kept private, but the grateful had let their stories out. It was well known and perhaps traded on, in hard times Matthew Conroy never took a fee. He was always on hand with free advice. He listened to people's problems when they came to him, tried to come up with solutions and most often did. Matthew Conroy had spent his life giving service to the community. All agreed he had been a wonderful father to his son. The proof was Jude himself.

No one seems to doubt I'm a winner, Jude thought. They don't know about the scars. The young woman Jude had seen slip into the church late—his hearing was so acute he could near hear a pin drop—was barely visible at the back. It was as though she had deliberately withdrawn into the shadows. Only her skin bloomed. It made him think of the creamy magnolias that grew in the front yard of his dad's house that now belonged to him. Whoever she was, he didn't recognise her. Intrigued, he turned his head slightly to take another look. Immediately she bent forward, her face downcast as if in prayer, or she'd realised her presence had drawn his interest and didn't welcome it.

By the time the service was over, she had disappeared. He even knew the moment she'd left. He thought he knew just about everyone in the town. Obviously she'd arrived fairly recently, or she was from out of town. He really couldn't understand why he was so curious. He certainly wasn't keeping watch on anyone else, not even poor little Mel, who had always wrung his heart.

Jude joined the slow, orderly, motorcade in the hire car Bobbi had organised to be waiting for him at the air terminal, some twenty kilometres from the town. It felt a little strange to be back to the snail's pace of his hometown. No traffic. No nightmare rush hour. No freeways, no one-ways. You could go wherever you wanted with no hassle at all. There was limitless peace and quiet, limitless golden sunlight to soak in, tropical heat and colour, white sand, and the glorious blue of the ocean at your door. The rain forest and the Great Barrier Reef were a jump away. Isis had been a wonderful place to grow up.

The family and the mourners—not everyone who had attended the service came—spread out around the gravesite, all slightly stunned Lester Rogan was actually dead and being lowered into the ground. He'd always seemed larger than life, a big, burly, commanding man with a voice like the rumble of thunder.

The interment took little time. The widow was a pitiable sight. Who knows what she was thinking. Ralph, sweating profusely, shovelled the first spadeful of dirt onto his father's ornate, gleaming casket with too much gusto. As Jude walked over to pay his respects to Myra and the family, he saw, not entirely to his surprise, the same young woman who had attracted his attention at the church. She was standing well away from the crowd, taking refuge and he suspected a degree of cover under the giant shade trees dotted all over the cemetery's well-tended grounds. There had to be a reason she was there. He could see she was taller than average, very slender. She wore a simple dark dress that managed to look amazingly chic, no hat, but a matching head scarf tied artfully. It completely covered her hair.

Who was she? He wondered if the family knew her. It didn't appear at all likely she was going to come across the grass to speak to them, unlike the other mourners who had formed themselves into a receiving line. They probably weren't relying on their memories of the late Lester in order to summon up a few kind words, Jude thought, his eyes still on the mystery woman.

Myra, to his surprise, reached up to kiss him as he offered his sympathies which were genuine for her and Mel. Many the time he'd heard Ralph wish his father dead. Melinda looked so lost and pathetic he took her into a comforting hug, allowing her head to nod against him.

"I'm so glad you're here, Jude," she whispered, deriving strength from her childhood friend's presence. Her own brother, Ralph, had been incredibly mean to her as a child.

Jude had always been nice to her and she'd never forget that.

"Anything I can do for you and your mother, Mel, I will," he was saying in his attractive voice. Melinda clung to Jude's arm, hanging on his every word.

"This must have been a big shock for you, Mel, even if your dad had health problems," Jude said.

"He didn't try at all," Mel lamented. "In fact you'd swear he was trying to kill himself. I couldn't love him, Jude. He wouldn't let me. You know that."

"He wasn't exactly fatherly material, Mel."

"Whereas your dad was everything a father should be," Mel sighed. "I know how cut up you were about losing your mother, Jude. You were very brave. But you had your dad and he was such a lovely man. My dad was very open about how stupid he thought we were." Melinda dabbed at her eyes with a lace edged handkerchief.

It had an old-fashioned scent like lavender. Heck, it was lavender, the sort old ladies bought. Jude found that a little strange for so young a woman.

Nevertheless he shook his head. "Never stupid, Mel." He comforted her. "You aren't and you know you aren't. It was just your father's way of trying to keep you all down."

"Well he succeeded." Melinda bowed her head like a sacrificial lamb. "Death is always a shock, even when you're half expecting it. He was my father, the most important person in my life. I feel a sense of awe he's gone. You're coming to the house aren't you?" Her soft grey eyes held a plea.

"Of course. I'm executor of your father's will. You do know that?"

"Ralph told us. I'm glad it's you, not a strange lawyer.

We really miss your father around here, Jude. He was very special. Like you.''

Jude gave a rueful smile. ''I'm not so special, Mel. I've got my faults just like the next guy. There'll be a reading whenever your mother feels up to it.''

Ralph, nearby, must have heard. He broke away from a group of mourners to stride up to them. ''Thanks for coming, Jude.'' The hard expression in his eyes didn't match his words. In fact he looked confrontational. Good old Ralph, still mired in his adolescent jealousies and resentments, Jude thought. ''It won't take long at the house before everyone starts moving off. I'd like you to read the will straight after.''

Jude glanced towards Myra doubtfully. ''Is that okay with your mother? She looks very frail.''

''It's okay with me,'' Ralph said tersely, turning on his heel again as though he was the only one who counted.

CHAPTER TWO

JUDE let the procession of mourners' cars get away before he made a move towards the hire car. As usual Ralph rubbed him up the wrong way as soon as he opened his mouth. Now he wanted to get the reading over before he returned to his family home. He'd taken Bobbi's advice and asked for his overdue vacation. Leonard Gooding had agreed on the spot, buoyed up by the fact Jude had managed to pull off a big, but complicated merger and in the process bring in new highly profitable business for the firm.

The path through the cemetery to the towering front gates was wide, but winding, flanked by enormous poincianas in full bloom. Their hectic blossoming had turned the very air rosy. The town cemetery was never a gloomy place even when the flowering was over. He should have had his eyes firmly on the drive but he happened to glance reflexively at his watch. When he looked up again, his heart skipped a beat, and every nerve ending tensed as he hit the brakes.

Right in front of him, a young woman was leaping back from the driveway to the grassy verge, her frozen expression betraying her shock at his car's near silent approach.

"Damn!" Within seconds he was out of the vehicle, watching in dismay as first she staggered then fell to the grass, thickly scattered with spent blossom. Her heel must have caught on something, he realized, probably an exposed root of one of the poincianas.

He had a sensation of falling himself. He was always a careful driver. There was no excuse. "Are you all right?"

Shoulders tensed, he bent to her, studying her with concern. "I'm so sorry. I didn't realise anyone was still about."

"My fault." Graciously, instead of berating him, she accepted his hand, wincing slightly as he brought her to her feet. "I shouldn't have been walking on the driveway at all. There are plenty of paths."

"Are you sure you're okay? You didn't injure your ankle?" They were a touch away but neither moved back.

"It'll be fine," she said quietly after a minute.

It was balm to his guilt. "That's a blessing." They both glanced down at her legs; classy legs on show in her short skirt. She wasn't wearing stockings in the heat, the skin tanned a pale gold. There was no swelling as far as he could see, but it could develop. "Jude Conroy," he said, holding out his hand.

"Cate Costello." She took his hand briefly, the expression in her beautiful green eyes not soft and lingering like the women's glances he was used to but quietly sizing him up.

"You're new in town?" He found himself staring back, all sorts of emotions crashing down on him like a wild surf. Up close she was even more lovely than his glimpse at the gravesite, like a vision from some tantalising dream. Her eyes had an unusual setting that bestowed an extra distinction on her delicate features. He realized straightaway she possessed an attraction that went beyond the physical though there was no denying that was potent enough.

There was the unblemished creamy skin he'd first noted in the church. Her large eyes, the feature that really stopped him in his tracks were a clear green, with a definite upward curve at the corners. The brows matched. Her face was a perfect oval, the finely chiselled contours off set by a contradictory mouth. The top lip was finely cut, the bottom surprisingly full and cushiony. Looking at her it was difficult not to dredge up the old cliché "English rose" but just as attractive to Jude was the keen intelligence in her regard.

He knew he was taking far too much time studying her, but she seemed quite unselfconscious under his scrutiny. She had to be around twenty two-or -three, but she seemed very self-contained for her age. Her voice, matched her patrician appearance; clear and well modulated. He wondered at the colour of her hair beneath the silk scarf and even found himself wanting to remove it. There was no question she had him in a kind of spell. Maybe it was the witchcraft of thc cycs? If he could keep talking to her until midnight maybe she would simply disappear?

As it was, she stood perfectly still, looking up at him, but he had the feeling she was equally well poised to run. "I've been here for six or seven months now," she said calmly in response to his question. "I know who you are."

Women habitually used that line with him. The old cynicism kicked in. "Really? Want to tell me how?"

"Anyone who comes to live in this town gets to know about you and your father," she explained matter-of-factly. "Your father was much loved and respected. You're the local celebrity."

He shrugged that off. "And you are?" Despite himself the words came out with the touch of steel he reserved for his job. Immediately he was aware of little sparks starting to fly between them. Whether they were harmful or not he couldn't yet say.

"I told you. Cate Costello." Her expression became intent as though she was deciding whether she liked or disliked him.

"Are you a friend of the family?"

She stepped back out of the brilliant sunlight into the shade. "Is this an interrogation, Jude Conroy?"

"Why would you see it that way, Ms Costello?" he countered, with a mock inclination of the head. "It's a perfectly normal question."

"If you'd said it in a different tone perhaps. Anyone can see you're a lawyer."

"You have a problem with lawyers?" He didn't bother to hide the challenge.

"I've never had occasion to call on one. But I appreciate they're necessary."

"I do believe so," he drawled. "And you, what do you do?" He made his tone friendly.

He was pouring on the charm, she thought, feeling tiny tremors ripple down her back. "Does it matter? We'll probably never see each other again."

He laughed, suddenly wanting nothing more than to get to know her better. "I can't help be curious."

"Well then," she relented, "I own a small gallery near the beach. It's called the Crystal Cave. I buy and sell crystals from all over the world."

"As in gazing?" Amusement showed in his gaze. He wasn't too far off in his assessment of her. "Obviously you don't have the slanted green eyes of a storybook witch for nothing."

A faint warning glitter came into those eyes. "I have no powers of clairvoyance, otherwise I'd have known you were a metre off running me over. I simply have a loving affinity with crystals."

"Ouch, I don't think I deserved that," he chided. "I braked immediately."

"I'm sorry." Her lovely face registered her sincerity.

"However did you start with your crystals?" An onlooker might have supposed they were good friends or even lovers so intent were they on each other.

"I knew some people who were great fossickers and collectors. They introduced me to the earth's treasures. I shared their love of gemstones and crystals. After all crystals have been used and revered since the beginning of civilisation.'' She looked away from him and those intensely blue searching eyes. The admiration in them was clearly flattering, but there was keen appraisal, too.

"So how can I find the Crystal Cave?" he asked. "I'm on vacation for a month."

"You intend to spend it here?" She looked back in surprise.

"Why not?" He slipped off his jacket, slinging it over his shoulder. "I was born in this town. I'll probably die here. You sound a little like you're wishing me on my way."

"Not at all." Colour rose to the cut-glass cheekbones. "It's I who should be on my way."

"On foot?" He took another look at her neat ankles. "Where's your car?"

"It's just around the corner." She gestured vaguely.

"Okay so I'll give you a lift. You're not going up to the house then?"

"The family don't know me, Mr Conroy."

"I'm fine with Jude," he told her. "I'm sure I'll find your gallery."

She made an attractive little movement with her hand. "That shouldn't be a problem. Everyone knows it. It used to be Tony Mandel's Art Gallery. The living quarters are at the rear. You'd have known Tony?"

"Of course I know Tony," he lightly scoffed. "He was a constant visitor at our house. My dad bought a number of his paintings in the early days before he became famous. I thought he was overseas."

She nodded. "He is. In London. His last showing was a sell-out. We keep in touch."

"So there's a connection?" Accustomed to asking questions, they were springing out.

"A family friend." Her smile conveyed she wasn't about to tell him more. "You really don't have to drive me. I can walk. It's not far."

"I insist. Can't have you hitchhiking." His speculative gaze lingered on her face.

"Why are you looking at me like that?" she questioned, with the tiniest frown.

"Forgive me, but I can't help wondering who you are and why you're at Lester Rogan's funeral when you don't know the family?"

She tilted her chin to look up at him. The knot in her stomach tightened. He had that confident demeanour tall men often have plus the superb body of an athlete. "Does it matter?" she asked, sounding a lot cooler than she felt.

"Damned if I haven't got the feeling it could."

"So you're the clairvoyant now." She smiled sweetly. "What's your astrological sign?" She restricted herself to a brief glance into his eyes. She'd heard he was dazzling, but in his favour he appeared unconcerned with his good looks. What she hadn't expected was the magnetism, the powerful attraction of that white, lopsided smile, the dimple that flicked deeply into his cheek.

"Leo," he was saying, still sounding indulgent, amused. "There's no scientific basis for astrology, Ms Costello."

The sapphire eyes were full of mischief. "I was going to tell you names of crystals you might find useful," she said coolly. "But no matter."

"Gee, thanks. That'd be fun," he lightly mocked. "Can you tell me something now?"

"If I can." She managed to sound at ease, even though the air around them was so sizzling it burned.

"What's the colour of your hair?" He could see he'd

caught her off guard. "I'm intrigued by your covering it up."

"Ever consider a bad hair day?" She cast him a quick glance.

"I'd be amazed if you were having one."

"It's obvious surely? I didn't particularly want to be noticed. But as you seem to be so curious."

Purposefully she raised a hand, lifting the silk scarf from her head. Another movement released the clasp at her nape.

He sucked in his breath sharply.

She shook her hair free, turning her head from side to side to loosen it. The breeze that swept along the driveway sent her hair swirling like a burnished veil. Sunlight reflected off myriad highlights like the prisms of a precious gem; gold, rose, amber, even pinks and orange. He supposed her long glorious mane would be best described as a gleaming copper.

"I can see what you mean about being noticed." Entranced, he nevertheless kept his tone sardonic. "You speak like the scarf was protection?"

She met his eyes again, tucking her hair casually behind her ears. The richness of the colour made her eyes and skin zing. "It doesn't do any harm to protect oneself. I really don't need a lift, you know. Thank you for the offer."

"No sense in walking in the heat. Deal?"

Her quick assessing glance skipped across his face again. "Okay."

They turned back towards the car. "As a copper-head it's a wonder your skin doesn't burn?" he asked conversationally, moving ahead to open the passenger door.

She slid in. "Strangely enough it doesn't, but I do use a good sunblock. The only hats I own were much too festive for a funeral."

"That's too bad. I'd like to have seen you in one." He

had a sudden mental image of her in a wide-brimmed hat weighed down with huge pink roses, something marvellously feminine and romantic. Ironically a hat like his mother used to wear to protect her skin. With a sudden twist of the heart he remembered how he'd fallen early and irrevocably in love with the image of a beautiful women in a picture hat. There were years when his parents had been passionate about their garden, working happily together. They'd even managed a beautiful sheltered rose garden, large, luxuriant shrubs and blooms, despite the humidity and attendant problems of the tropics. To this day he took a lot of pleasure out of sending roses to his dates.

It wasn't until Jude had dropped the mysterious Cate Costello off at her car that he realized she still hadn't revealed what exactly she was doing at Lester Rogan's funeral.

Ten minutes later he arrived at the Rogan mansion, the overt display of the late Lester Rogan's wealth. The house was huge. In his view no architectural gem but impressive for sheer size alone and the tropical splendour of the five acre manicured grounds. The entrance was electronically guarded, the long driveway lined by majestic Royal Cuban palms. A caretaker-gardener's bungalow was off to the left through the screening trees. There was a pool and a guest-house at the back, but surpassing all the obvious signs of wealth, was the glorious blue sea.

There were plenty of cars littering the driveway and the grass. Jude found a spot, his mind still engaged with his meeting with Cate Costello. What could possibly have motivated her to attend Rogan's funeral if she didn't know the family? Or could he take that to mean she just didn't know Myra, Ralph and Melinda, but she had known Lester? In what context? Lester could have bought out Tony Mandel's beachside property that was the most obvious connection. These days with tourism in tropical North Queensland hectically blossoming the land would be very valuable for redevelopment at some future date. If the late Lester had been her landlord, why didn't she say so? What was the big mystery? What was she doing sheltering amid the trees? He hadn't the slightest doubt he'd find out.

An hour later hurried along by a less than subtle Ralph, all the mourners had departed, some of them definitely over the drink driving limit.

"Now's as good a time as any to read the will," Ralph rasped. "You've got it with you?" He threw Jude an impatient glance.

"Of course. I left my briefcase in the hall."

"I'll get it Jude," Melinda offered. She was nearest the wide archway, one of a pair that led from off the entrance hall to the major reception rooms.

"Sure you're up to this, Mrs Rogan?" Jude asked, taking another concerned look at Myra's extreme pallor. "I can very easily come back tomorrow, or the next day."

Ralph's dark eyes shot red sparks of aggression. Here was a young man who was permanently angry. "For cryin' out loud, Jude, how many times do I have to tell you? We're ready to hear it? Right now."

The school bully was still holding up. "I was talking to your mother, Ralph. Not you." Unperturbed Jude looked towards Myra who was giving every appearance of being the next to follow her husband to the grave.

"Mum tell him." Ralph scratched his forehead violently.

"No, Ralphie—no." Myra pleaded, her voice tremulous.

Ralph stared at his mother for a bit, giving a can-you-believe-this roll of his eyes. "Listen," he said very quietly as though addressing someone mentally challenged. "This won't take long then you can take to your bed. For the rest of your life if you like.''

"I think she needs her bed right now," Jude said, trying to keep the disgust out of his voice. "This has been a bad shock.''

"Get it over with, Jude," Melinda advised, returning with his briefcase. In her own way she appeared as eager to hear the will as her brother. "I'll look after Mum. She's stronger than she looks. Dad hammered away at her for years."

"Yes, get it over, Jude," Myra's opposition suddenly collapsed, as if she thought both her children were about to ostracize her.

"Okay." Against his better judgment Jude deferred to their wishes. "Mel, you might like to settle your mother in a more comfortable chair." Myra was perched like a budgie on the edge of a small antique chair that looked like it was only good for decoration.

Melinda put her arm around her mother, leading her to an armchair. Myra took her time, her movements those of a woman twenty years her senior. Jude suspected Dr Atwell had given her medication to get her through the service. She was pretty much out of it. Meanwhile, Ralph was shaping up to be as nasty as his late father.

"Sit the hell down, Mum," Ralph confirmed Jude's assessment by crying out in utter exasperation.

"You're awful, Ralph," his sister croaked, as if she couldn't get past the big lump of misery in her throat. "A real pig."

"Like Dad." Ralph looked back at her out of his deepset dark eyes. "Okay, Mr Hotshot, read the will."

Jude stepped right up to him, two inches taller, a stone or more lighter, but obviously fitter by far. "Jude will do, thanks, Ralph, and a little more respect all around. I'm your late father's lawyer, not your lackey." Jude didn't give a damn about how much money the Rogans had. Never had. It showed in the sapphire glitter of his eyes.

"So take it easy." Swaying slightly from side to side, Ralph backed off. "Surely you can understand I'm anxious to hear how Dad left things between the three of us."

"Of course." Jude took a seat in the armchair nearest the big Oriental style coffee table so he could put the document down to read it. He withdrew the will from his briefcase, the collective eyes of the family trained on him. They wouldn't be seeing shades of his father. Jude bore little physical resemblance to him, apart from his height. He even had his mother's dimple in his left cheek just so he could never forget her.

"Hang on a moment I'll get myself a drink. Anyone else want one?" Ralph lumbered off looking over his shoulder.

"Haven't you had enough, Ralph?" Myra roused herself sufficiently to ask.

Ralph snorted. "Been countin', Ma?" He poured himself a generous shot of whiskey from a spirits laden trolley, tonging a couple of ice cubes into it. "You, Jude?"

"Thank you. No." As instructed, Jude wanted to get on with it, his expression as professional as any lawyer's could get.

Ralph positioned himself on the opposite side of the coffee table, swirling the amber contents of his crystal tumbler, hunkering down his broad shoulders.

Jude showed them Lester Rogan's will with the seal intact. He viewed their faces intently, then he broke open the long, thick envelope, beginning to read with suitable gravitas...

"This is the last will and testament of me, Lester Michael Rogan..."

Instantly he was interrupted by Myra's stricken cry, one of many to be ripped from her throat. Was this for real?

Jude agonised, wanting to shake his head in amazement. She had no reason to love her husband. Mel grabbed her mother's hand and held it. It didn't appear to be a gesture of comfort, more to shut her mother up.

"Would you mind keeping a lid on it, Ma. Is that too much to ask?" Ralph slewed another disgusted look at his mother. "Continue, Jude."

Jude continued, managing from experience to keep his voice perfectly level despite the rippling shock he felt. "This will is to be held in terrorem," he announced, looking up for a reaction.

"What the hell's that? I haven't a clue." Ralph waved his glass, empty now except for a melting ice cube.

It means this will is going to be one big surprise, Jude thought without immediately responding. Any member of the family who contested Lester Rogan's wishes could finish up with nothing. Ralph pre-set to take over his father's real estate empire was visibly disturbed.

"Why don't you let me read on," Jude suggested. "I'll explain all the legal jargon later."

"Fine," Ralph muttered through gritted teeth.

"This relates to disposition of property," Jude advised them. "To my wife, Myra..." Not the usual beloved, that would have been too much to ask. This highly dysfunctional family knew little about love, Jude thought. It took five seconds for Myra to let out another agonized wail this one so sharp Jude winced. Both of her children however ignored her, continuing to stare fixedly at Jude. "To my wife, Myra," Jude started off again, "I bequeath sole possession of the family home, land and all the contents therein plus the adjoining five acres. In addition she is to receive the sum of ten million dollars which should allow her to see out her days comfortably. In the unlikely event she remarry, the house and all land reverts to my son, Ralph. Myra can do what she likes with the contents.''

Ralph made a dramatic grasp at his heart. He had expected his mother was due for heaps more. Lester had to be worth around $85 to $100 million. Everyone knew he'd been shovelling money in! Wasn't Myra legally entitled to a sizeable percentage of the estate? Ralph wasn't sure. What he was sure of was she wouldn't put up a fight. More for him. Like his dad, Ralph couldn't seriously believe another man would lavish love on his mother.

Jude continued. ''To my daughter, Melinda—'' again no expression of affection, this was becoming a habit ''—I bequeath an annual income of seventy-five thousand dollars to be paid from the trust established for this purpose. The payments will continue up until such time as she marries. On her wedding day she will receive as final payment five million dollars.'' No gifts, no mementos, not even a pair of Lester's favourite cuff links. What code had Lester stuck to?

Peanuts, Ralph was thinking, a triumphant laugh escaping him. ''Mean old bastard.'' That only meant one thing. He was the big winner. At long last after all these years of humiliation he was going to score big time. He'd have control of everything. As long as he lived he'd never have to take anything from another living soul. He was powerful. Rich. Ralph's bloodshot eyes began to gleam. He could buy and sell Golden Boy Conroy.

''To my son, Ralph, named after a man he couldn't in any way hold a candle to, I bequeath my collection of sporting trophies and motor cars, my motor yacht, *Sea Eagle*, my portrait by Dargy in the study and the sum of five million dollars in the hope he can do something with himself in the future.'' Jude glanced up. The tension in the room was so thick he could have cut it with a knife.

"Go on, go on." Ralph jumped to his feet as though he'd been attacked with an ice pick. "There's more. There's gotta be more. I'm the heir!"

"Of course there's more, dear," Myra consoled him, albeit fearfully, the pale skin of her face and neck mottled red.

"Of course there's more," Melinda chimed in, characteristically satisfied with her lot. "Please sit down again. Go on, Jude."

Jude felt a certain tightness in his chest. He didn't want to say this. "To Jude Kelsey Conroy, son of the only man I've ever trusted, Matthew John Conroy, a most honourable man, and in recognition of Jude's devotion to his father and his own outstanding merits I bequeath the sum of one hundred thousand dollars knowing he will use it wisely. The residue of my estate, land, houses, rental properties, share portfolio I hereby bequeath to Catherine Elizabeth Costello, spinster, of the…"

Whatever else Jude, more dismayed than pleased with his windfall, was about to say, it was cut off by Ralph's bull roar. It would have been pretty scary to a lot of people.

Jude wasn't one of them. "Do you want to hear the rest of this, Ralph?" he asked crisply. "I should say I knew nothing of my bequest."

"When your dad drew it up?" Ralph snarled with a curl of the lip. "I bloody well *don't* want to hear any more of this." He picked up his crystal tumbler and hurled it across the living room where it smashed to smithereens against a large bronze sculpture of a rodeo rider atop a bucking horse. Rage, shock, contempt was written across his face.

"Did the old fool go mad?" he demanded of them all, though no one came up with an answer. "Catherine Elizabeth Costello. Who is she? Some fancy whore he had on the side? What hold did she have on him? I can't believe this. It's like my worst nightmare. Who is this woman? The woman he wanted to marry? Not Ma?''

Jude was struggling hard to master his own shock. Now he knew for certainty that Cate Costello and trouble went together. He stared at each member of the family in turn. ''Do none of you know her?''

Myra shook her head vigorously. At least she seemed to have snapped out of her catatonic state.

''I know of her,'' Melinda admitted, staring at Jude. She looked the very picture of bewilderment, which seemed to be her general condition. ''She runs a gallery, the Crystal Cave, near the beach.''

''What does that have to do with us?'' Ralph bellowed, reaching down for his father's will with the obvious intention of tearing it to bits.

Jude swiftly removed it from harm's way, while Ralph glared at him. ''You knew about this?'' he demanded.

Jude shook his head ready to give Ralph a good shove if he decided to get nasty. Not that he altogether blamed him. Who was Catherine Elizabeth Costello and what had she been to Lester Rogan? ''You saw me break the seal. I'm as shocked as you are.'' For various reasons he didn't announce to the family he had already met Rogan's heiress. One of them was to protect her, another was to avoid getting into a fistfight with Ralph. Ralph in this mood was as destructive as a boxer with a sore head.

''She's young,'' Melinda frowned hard in concentration, gripping her mother's hand as if it might assist her recollections. ''Younger than I am. She's beautiful. She has the most wonderful hair. The colour's sort of indescribable, redgold. I've seen her in the town any number of times but we've never actually met.''

''She moved here,'' Ralph growled, banging his muscular arms together. ''I remember now. The chick at Mandel's old place. I've had her description from quite a few of the guys. To think I meant to check her out when I had the time! Dad saw I had as little spare time as possible. I don't get this? What would a good-looking young chick have to do with my big ugly geriatric dad?''

Myra whistled indignation through her nostrils. ''No one could have called your father old or ugly,'' she burst out, in her loyal, long-suffering wife mode. ''He wasn't even sixty. Sixty these days is young I might remind you. Your father was handsome as you're handsome but you'd better lose some weight. And very soon. I'm amazed you can still get into your clothes. For Heaven's sake, Jude,'' She turned her attention away from her near apoplexic son. ''You have to advise us. This has taken us all by shock. You're telling me Lester has left the bulk of his estate to a young woman none of us knows?''

''That's it, Mrs Rogan.'' Jude threw up his hands. ''I don't understand what's happened here. I confidently expected the estate to be divided between the family. I have no idea why your husband did what he did, but as the appointed executor of your late husband's estate, I promise you I'll find out. I have my responsibilities.''

''You bet you do!'' Ralph dredged up a lifetime of jealousy and irritation. He was breathing hard through his large, straight nose, making a surprisingly loud whistling noise. ''I always knew my dad was a mean bastard. I never figured he was a lunatic as well. He's shafted me. He's shafted the whole family. Even when he's dead he's punishing us.'' The destruction of his hopes and dreams was written all over Ralph's face. ''He won't get away with it. The money is rightfully mine.''

''Ours,'' Melinda piped up to keep the record straight. ''Mum's.''

''What the hell would you two know to do with it?''

Ralph glared at his sister, standing up to get himself another drink. "You and Ma know nothing about business. You've spent your life on your backsides. He mightn't have loved you but you had everything else you wanted. You never even had the guts, Mel, to find yourself a job. How many chicks your age haven't actually had a job? Anyone would think you couldn't read or write."

"You can stop that now, Ralph," Myra admonished in an astonishingly severe voice. "I needed Mel at home."

"So both of you could watch the flowers grow?" Ralph threw back his head and laughed. "Ah hell!" He reached out in extreme frustration sending a pile of glossy magazines flying. "You're the big shot lawyer, Conroy, what's your advice?"

"Nice of you to ask me, Ralph. The will would only be invalid if your father had been of unsound mind when he made it," Jude pointed out in a deceptively calm voice. "As far as I know there wouldn't be a soul around who could prove he was. Your mother has rights by law, family home, etc. In that regard, she's been provided for. You and Mel don't actually have rights as such, Ralph. Your father was free to do as he liked with his money. You and Mel have been provided for. In terrorem means in layman's language if any of you contest the will you'll get nothing."

Ralph executed a full turn, swearing violently. He slammed his fist down on the mahogany coffee table, the steam of anger rising off him. "What if the old devil was insane? What if this girl had him wound around her little finger? What if she bamboozled him into making the will in her favour? I wish I knew where she came from."

That makes two of us Jude thought. "You could contest the will on that basis, Ralph," he offered a legal opinion, actually feeling sorry for the guy. "Work the duress angle. But I'm duty-bound to tell you legal proceedings could risk your inheritance. What's more, your mother has first claim on the estate. If you wanted to fight it your mother has to initiate the action. She could lose. That would be a terrible result. What I have to do is meet with this young woman and establish the connection.''

"Even your dad, that honourable man, betrayed us.'' Ralph looked across at Jude with open hostility.

Jude's whole body tensed. "Don't bring my father into this, Ralph. You'd better know right now I won't stand for it. My father carried out your father's wishes.''

"Shame on you, Ralph.'' Melinda's soft voice turned shrill with rebuke. "You know the respect Dad had for Mr Conroy. Dad was always interested in Jude, too. Dad put a lot of store in brains.''

"You were behind the door when they were handed out,'' Ralph taunted his sister. He turned his glance back on Jude. "I bet your dad told you all about it.''

"I've got a couple of things to say, Ralph.'' Jude, who'd had just about enough of Ralph even given the years in-between, looked at him out of steely eyes. "Mel was actually considered a good student, remember? She got good grades.'' He never added "unlike you'' but it hung in the air. "My father said nothing whatever to me.'' Jude stood up, quietly returning the time bomb of a will to his briefcase before snapping it shut. "It's called lawyer-client privilege. My father was absolutely clear about his role. I'm very sorry, believe me, your father's will wasn't what you all wanted, and confidently expected. As your father's executor I have to pay Ms Costello a visit.''

"Just be sure you report back to us straight away,'' Ralph threw up his big head belligerently.

"I'm not your lawyer, Ralph,'' Jude pointed out. "I act as executor for your late father's estate.'' He turned to Myra, his hand out, a sympathetic smile in his eyes. "As a family friend, Mrs Rogan, if you do wish to retain me I'll do everything in my power to help you.''

Myra stood up, still holding his hand. ''Thank you so much, Jude. We do need your help. My boy needs help. I can't take all this in. Everything has been such a shock.''

''I can appreciate that, Mrs Rogan.'' And how!

''I'll walk you to the door, Jude,'' Melinda offered catching hold of Jude's arm. ''I'm so glad you're here for us. I guess we'll find out soon enough what this Catherine Costello was to Dad.''

What indeed! Jude felt all kinds of horrors creep along his skin. He and Cate Costello were strangers though they had spoken briefly. Nevertheless he wasn't sure he could deal with the possibility she might have been Lester Rogan's mistress. It wasn't as though such things didn't happen. Rich powerful men, even geriatrics as Ralph had suggested, didn't have much of a problem picking up female trophies. But how could a young woman so beautiful and seemingly so refined as Cate Costello be part of anything so totally ugly? The very idea didn't so much disgust as numb him. Life was so complicated. He doubted he would ever reach a period in life when it wasn't.

CHAPTER THREE

HE DIDN'T mean to deal with the issue today. He wanted time to think about the whole situation at least overnight.

He went home. Jude focused his gaze on the high beach road that was the quickest route to his house at Spirit Cove some three miles from the Rogan mansion. The narrow road, divided by a white line down the middle, clung on one side to the glorious blue ocean; on the other, beyond an open space of lush tropical vegetation were the plantations; sugar cane, banana, mango, pineapple, avocado, new species of tropical fruits some of which he'd never even tasted.

The town had grown, extending much further south along the coast road and up the low indigo hills of the hinterland. The hills, tropical rain forests, were full of beautiful birds, gorgeous parrots, and plants. There were tree dwelling orchids, the dendrobium, the state flower of Queensland, spider orchids, angel orchids, terrestrial orchids, the extraordinary bromeliads with their vividly coloured centre leaves. He knew all those hills. He had explored them as a boy.

The golden disc of the sun was hot and brilliant. There was a bluish haze over the water. Blue water all around, glittering as if a billion metallic sequins had been cast on the rolling surface. Blue sky above. This was the tropics. Ineffable gold and blue.

He'd lowered the passenger window so the sea breeze could waft in. It bore the fragrance of sea water and salt mingled with the tropical fruits that grew nearby and the delicious scent of flowers. The lovely frangipani that grew everywhere in profusion, the common cream-yellow-centred flowers and nowadays almost as many pink and red. There were frangipanis twenty feet high in his home garden and the scent when they were in flower was so exquisitely heady as to be near unbearable. The frangipani were as ubiquitous as the indestructible oleanders of many colours that massed in great numbers around the cove where he was heading.

As he drove he could see draped over every fence and outbuilding a spectacular array of flowering vines; golden trumpets blazing away, the flashy Morning Glory, jasmines in flower all year round, allamandas and black-eyed Susans, the flame vines and the giant solandras. One had to be very careful planting vines in the tropics. They had a habit of running rampant, in no time at all turning into impenetrable jungle.

At least the lush beauty all around him was calming his thoughts. They'd been heading off in all directions, mostly centred on the mystery woman, Cate Costello. She'd fooled him with her clear direct gaze.

He couldn't bear to think of her as Lester Rogan's mistress. For that matter he couldn't bear to think of any man's hands on her which didn't exactly make sense. He didn't even know her. Was it possible there was a biological tie to Rogan? There was no evidence of it in her appearance. She bore no physical resemblance whatsoever to him—no single feature, eyes, mouth, nose, chin let alone the hair colour. Could she possibly be Rogan's long-lost illegitimate daughter? She'd told him she didn't know the family. She'd lied. She definitely knew Lester Rogan. That was a bad start.

He remembered those beautiful eyes, their cool green colour emphasized by her delicate dark brows and thick eyelashes, startling given the copper hair. Maybe that cascade of glowing silk was dyed? Women changed their hair colour all the time. There were lots of things he had yet to learn about Cate Costello. So far he'd learned she was hiding a great deal.

As had the late Lester Rogan, real estate tycoon. Why? His career wouldn't have suffered had he acknowledged paternity of a child other than his son, Ralph and his daughter Melinda. His wife, Myra, was so completely dominated she wouldn't have given him a terrible time had he confided in her or simply produced a surprise offspring as a fait accompli.

Jude groaned aloud. Lester Rogan wasn't her father. He couldn't be. He wouldn't believe it. Wouldn't his own father have known? His dad was one of the few people Lester Rogan had ever been known to confide in.

So what was the story? He let his mind range over a half a dozen scenarios all of which he hated. Surely he hadn't let a complete stranger get under his skin? He wasn't ready for that kind of connection with any woman much less one who gazed into crystal balls. He was depressed, too that she had lied to him. He hated lies.

Minutes later he arrived home. An old fishing mate of his father's, Jimmy Dawson, though not a caretaker as such— Jimmy had his own little bungalow on the edge of the rain forest—kept the grounds under control. At least the jungle hadn't set in. He got out to open the white picket gates, looking up with deep nostalgia at the handsome white house that stood tall against the turquoise sky. This was his much loved home right up until the time he had started his legal career in the state capital. Two storied it was surrounded by wide verandahs with a green painted galvanised roof and glossy emerald-green shutters to protect the pairs of French doors along the verandahs in times of tropical storms. A wide flight of six steps led to the porch.

His mother had always kept two huge ceramic pots planted with masses of white flowers flanking the double doorway with its beautiful stained-glass transom. Towering palms stood in the large, very private grounds, the lawns a carpet of lush green. Obviously Jimmy had seen to the mowing. The wonderfully spectacular poincianas were in full bloom as were the flame trees. On either side of the house the magnolias carried great plate-sized blooms, creamy-white and resplendent over the rich dark green leaves burnished underneath.

The flower beds had not survived although agapanthus, strelitzias, cannas, cassias and gardenias had gown back to the wild. The long fences on either side of the house were totally taken over by a dense screen of King Jasmine. Jude supposed the timber had rotted, teetering beneath the rampant vines which were so strong they were virtually self-supporting. It would be getting too much for Jimmy even with help. Jimmy was much older than Jude's father, around seventy but wonderfully fit and wiry or he had been the last time Jude had seen him about a year ago. A year at Jimmy's time of life was a long time.

He had rung Jimmy to let him know he was coming. The house had been aired. There was milk, butter, cheddar cheese, bacon and eggs, a whole roasted chicken, a bottle of chardonnay, four jars of cumquat marmalade in the frig—cumquat marmalade, brandied cumquats, pickled cumquats, you name it, cumquats were the base of Jimmy's home made specialties—Jimmy like his dad didn't bother growing the miniature fruit in pots like some people. He grew them in long hedges as a windbreak, always teeming with fruit or flower. Jude looked in the bread bin, found a fresh loaf. There was tea and coffee in the pantry, a few more groceries and a bottle of whiskey—he laughed at that.

Jimmy was a great guy, an honourary uncle to him when he was growing up. His throat tightened with affection and gratitude. Jimmy had been organised to go fishing with his dad that terrible day only another friend of Jimmy's had stumbled over a snake on his way home from the pub and got bitten for his trouble. Jimmy, being a drinker, was on hand to get his friend to the hospital. The rest was history.

"Anyone at home?" he called to the empty house, knowing he would never again get the answer he wanted. "Are you there, Dad?" Would he ever get over the loss! His heart gave a little jump as one of the mahogany treads on the staircase that led off the entrance hall creaked loudly. Doubtless his father still walked around the house. "Dad, do you know how I miss you." Jude continued to talk to himself as he prowled around.

What better place for his father to roam than Spirit Cove. There was an off-beat story as to why the cove had been so named. Some sixty years before, a pretty young woman of the town, known to be head over heels in love with a married man, the owner of one of the district's largest sugar plantations, had drowned herself there. A lot of people over the years claimed they saw her at night walking along the beach. She was always wearing flimsy white draperies that billowed in the sea breeze. Jimmy who loved telling a good yarn claimed he'd once got close enough to talk to her before she dematerialised before his very eyes. Oddly Jude's highly sceptical mother claimed to have seen her once. Jude remembered her shock had been real.

It only added to the atmosphere. As a boy, alone or with a friend staying over, he'd stolen onto the star spangled beach. Much as he wanted the thrill of seeing a ghost he'd seen nothing and not been surprised.

Jude started to roam through the house with its large rooms that flowed into each other and led to the huge deck his parents had used constantly for entertaining when he was growing up. He loved this area with its beautiful views of the ocean. One lived outdoors in the tropics.

The rear garden was crowded with fruit trees. Mango, banana, avocado, fig, luminous golden lemons, limes, custard apples, pineapple guavas. No one would go hungry here. There used to be deep vegetable gardens, an endless supply of sweet little cherry tomatoes he would pop into his mouth. But no more. Sometimes in his dreams he saw his parents working happily together in the garden like they used to, his mother's beautiful face protected by one of her big straw sunhats. Those were the days when they'd been a happy family. Or so he'd thought. In reality his mother had probably been planning her getaway.

Why dream of his mother when he'd never had a conversation with her after age twelve. He had no idea what had happened to her. No doubt her second marriage to a rich man had worked out well—always supposing the rich American had married her. He could have half sisters and brothers for all he knew. He would acknowledge any siblings but never his mother. She'd left his father alone to grieve; turned him marriage-shy. To love was to lose. Jude shoved off the clinging threads of desolation.

Settled in or as settled as he could get, he rang Jimmy to thank him, inviting him over next day. Maybe they could go into town he proposed? Have lunch at the excellent little pub? Extraordinarily restless, he pushed through the picket gate to walk down to the beach with its pristine white sand.

The dunes were swathed in succulents with gossamer thin yellow flowers. Swaying coconut palms, some bent at odd angles by the force of the wind, and spiky pandanus threw shadows over the beach. At this time of the afternoon the sea was a rich royal-blue. The ocean had as many facets as gemstones, sometimes sapphire, emerald turquoise, now tanzanite. North of Capricorn was such a beautiful part of the world, the light incandescent. He kicked off his shoes feeling the familiar crunch of sand beneath his feet. He had lots to think about. Jude found his way down to the hard sand near the water's edge.

He settled for a plate of chicken sandwiches and a pot of coffee for supper, eating it out on the rear deck. By seven o'clock he started to feel he should have called on Cate Costello that afternoon instead of leaving it until tomorrow. He was seriously annoyed with himself for getting into a spin about a girl he didn't even know. He was behaving right out of character.

Ten minutes later he took to the road, driving into town. He had every excuse to drop in on her. Perhaps he should have rung but then she might have taken the opportunity to slip out. She had recognised him easily enough. She knew he was Jude Conroy, a lawyer. It would be a simple matter for a smart young woman like her to put two and two together and realize he was here for the will reading. She said she didn't know the family but she hadn't been able to stay away from Lester Rogan's funeral. She had deceived him and he dealt with totally convincing liars every day of the week. There seemed little doubt she'd known Lester. Probably when he was in town one day habitual womaniser Lester had stepped into the shop and seen her there among all her pretty glittering crystals, the creamy skin, the long copper hair, the up tilted green eyes. Jude had heard the old myths from Ireland about how red-haired women had ''the powers.''

Powers or not, she was a man-trap if ever there was one. As Myra had said, the late Lester Rogan could hardly be described as old or unattractive. He'd been a big, vigorous imposing looking man, larger than life, quite out of the ordinary. All through his married life it was an open secret he took mistresses, but never as young as twenty-two or thereabouts. They were usually thoroughly respectable widows and the like. The youngest Jude could recall, a schoolteacher who had quietly been moved on after an anonymous letter to the Education Department, was around thirty-six. His father had always said mildly, ''Les is fond of the women!'' Boy, what an understatement! The late Lester Rogan had had no idea what it meant to be faithful, but he could provide his women with the finer things in life. Women were big on such things!

Either Ms Catherine Elizabeth Costello had well and truly come off her pedestal or there was some piece of the puzzle Jude hadn't yet hit on. There was no getting away from it mistress seemed the most likely scenario given Lester's predilections.

When he arrived at the Crystal Cave, the site of Tony Mandel's old art gallery, he saw the place in a pool of semi-darkness. He contemplated it briefly. Little had changed. It wasn't until he got out of the car that he spotted the red sports car nosed right in to the grove of golden canes at the far side of the building. Instantly all the muscles under his skin tightened.

Ralph! It was enough to make the knees buckle. Anger and a kind of panic hit him. When he'd left the Rogan mansion that afternoon Ralph had been drunk. Why hadn't he considered bully-boy Ralph, the hothead, might take it upon himself to come out to where she lived? An awful image flashed into his mind of the girl trying to grapple with a drink inflamed Rogan.

Jude, the athlete, moved with speed, running along the narrow side of the house to the rear garden. His heart was pounding up into his throat, betraying his agitation. Why hadn't he called her? Then he would have known Ralph was there. He prayed that Ralph had only just arrived. Ralph at the best of times had a short fuse, drunk he would be ugly and unpredictable. Eaten away with bitterness and resentment from a lifetime of hoarding up every little snub, every little slight robbed of his inheritance he would be positively dangerous.

The back of the house was well lit. All the exterior lights were on, flooding the deck with its vaulting canopy of flowering poinciana and shining out into the small square of lawn densely planted around the perimeter by a hedge of gardenia bushes. Coconut palms whispered in the cooling breeze, a sensuous sound for once he didn't hear. He caught a great gust of perfume from the richly seductive gardenia, the hundreds and hundreds of white flowers illuminated by the strong security lights.

He was almost at the steps when a night bird darted low over his head startling him but it was nothing like the freezing shock he received when a young urgent cry issued from inside the house.

"Get out! Go away! Please…just go!" It was a cry that imparted fear, intimidation and loathing.

Jude took the flight of steps two at a time, contemplating what he might do to Ralph and to hell with the consequences. Lawyers weren't supposed to get into fistfights, but just let him get his hands on Ralph. His face was rigid with anger and disgust. Ralph Rogan would never change. He wouldn't know how to.

What he saw through the picture windows was a long comfortably furnished room divided into open kitchen and living area. The girl was stumbling back from a menacing Rogan, one of her arm's held up defensively like a shield. Ralph was advancing slowly, but his resolve to manhandle her was sickeningly apparent. The girl's hands plucked at a chair as if she thought to defend herself with it. Her hair spilled copper over a low-neck top that revealed the cleft between her breasts. She wore white shorts, no shoes. She'd been thoroughly at home at her beach house before Ralph arrived. Very soon he'd be on her. She looked as delicate and breakable as a lily on a stalk, absolutely no match for Ralph.

Jude felt the blood rush to his head. He saw Rogan reach for her with his long, powerful arms—he'd never quite realised how big Ralph was until he saw how he dwarfed this girl. He saw Ralph miss her altogether as she retreated on nimble feet, four feet away, this time straining for something to throw. There was the expected fear of a victim in her face—Ralph was a daunting sight—but a courageous defiance, too. Jude recognised she meant to put up a fight. Ralph would recognise it, too, only Ralph would relish it. It would be an opportunity for him to show his power. Her beauty and vulnerability would only serve to increase the lusty sexual appetite Ralph had inherited from his father.

Jude felt a great surge of adrenaline. He threw back the door so violently it had the effect of a gunshot. At the impact both people inside the room were stopped in their tracks. The girl stared at him. She was all eyes—burning emeralds in a milk-white face. Ralph was twisting his big body unsteadily in an effort to confront the invader, his ugly expression abruptly turning furtive.

"Had to be you, Conroy!" he rasped, his voice lifting in volume. "Always rushing to a lady's defence. What do ya—?"

He broke off open-mouthed, as the girl went flying across the room as graceful as a ballerina, her hair a bright turbulence around her. She backed up beside Jude, clearly for protection.

"Thank God you're here!" she gasped. "You saved me."

He wasn't ready to forgive her, in fact he felt unaccountably angry with her. "Perhaps you can tell me why the hell you let him in?" He felt for her hand, hauled her protectively to his side.

Cate recognised the fury in his blazing blue eyes. "I didn't let him in. I was adamant he couldn't come in, but he shoved me back inside. Pulled the door shut. There was no reasoning with him."

"You know him, don't you?" He didn't look at her but there was hard accusation in Jude's tone.

"Know him?" Cate stared across at the coarsely handsome Ralph who now appeared stupefied by the turn of events. "I know of him. He's Ralph Rogan. I've never actually met him until tonight."

"Well, this isn't my idea of coming courting," Jude clipped off, his natural sweetness of manner totally lost. "Caught you, you miserable bastard," he addressed Ralph in a chilling low voice. "Just what were you intending?" Jude took the opportunity to move the girl out of harm's way before starting across the space that divided him from Ralph.

Ralph awkwardly backed up, Jude's anger cutting into him like a blade. "Listen, Jude, I've no argument with you," he blustered, continuing to inch away. "I wanted answers from her. Can you blame me?"

"Harassment isn't the way to go about it." Jude gritted.

Ralph found his breath quickening. He'd learned his lesson years ago, he didn't want to tangle with Conroy in this mood. "She played Dad for a fool," he blurted. "You know that. I wanted her to tell me."

"Don't keep backing up, Ralph," Jude taunted. "I'm itching to take you apart. You never learn do you?"

"What good would that do?" Ralph asked, shifting his body yet again to prevent his muscles seizing. "Aren't you supposed to be our lawyer?"

Cate realized she had to stop this. She moved swiftly, rushing forward to put herself between the two men.

"Don't." Her green eyes pleaded with Jude. "He's not worth it."

"Would you mind getting out of the way?" Jude kept his eyes on the unpredictable Ralph. Ralph could yet try something, but Jude would be ready.

"This is my place," Cate said, not budging an inch. "I don't want to see you get into a fight over me. I want him to leave."

Jude's golden-blond head slowly turned until he met her eyes. "You don't want to ring the police?"

"I want him to leave," Cate repeated, refusing to surrender to tears of relief. "He's mad. He said he was going to set the place on fire. He said he was going to drive me out of town."

"You said that did you, Ralph?" Jude asked in a dead-flat voice. "Ring the police. You can bring charges." He risked another glance at the girl.

"You better not try." Ralph's deep-set eyes glittered malignantly as he made his gruff threat. "Damn you, Conroy. Whose side are you on anyway?" he demanded. "Why didn't you do what you were supposed to do? Why didn't you get the full story out of this little whore?"

Red spots flamed in Cate's cheeks. "I'd be very careful what you say," she said tightly. "For that, I will report you. I'm going to ring right now." She moved with quiet determination. "You can explain yourself to them, you horrible pig." She moved towards the kitchen where she picked up the portable phone on the counter.

"Don't do it," Ralph burst out sharply. "Put it down. Tell her, Jude. I don't want any fuss here."

Jude gave a hard, disbelieving laugh. "On the contrary I'm advising her to ring. I'm a witness. I saw you menacing her and I believe you were about to physically assault her."

Ralph's strong legs abruptly turned to syrup. He crashed

into a chair, wiping his sweating brow with the back of his hand. "Stop her, Jude. I swear I wasn't going to do anything, I was just trying to talk to her. I had no idea she would panic so badly. She went a lot wilder than she's trying to make out."

Hatred was alive and burning inside of Ralph, Jude was sure of it, but so was the bully-boy back-off he remembered from the past.

"I'm sorry. I didn't mean to scare you." Ralph said to Cate, his dark face blotchy with drink and rage. "I apologise."

Cate put the phone down slowly, nibbling hard on her lip. She was a newcomer in town and she had a business to run. She didn't want any scandals if she could help it. "I'm certain you did mean to scare me." She contradicted him flatly. She could have added she feared he wouldn't have stopped at rape. There'd been something feral in his eyes. She'd seen eyes like that before. "There's a small matter of your breaking in," she reminded him. "I was off guard. You flung me away, sent me sprawling. Your purpose was to frighten and intimidate. I shudder to think what might have happened had Jude not arrived."

There was a crazed sparkle in Ralph's eyes. "Jude?" He eyed one then the other. "You two know one another?"

"No, we don't," Jude denied it flatly. "You've been calling me Jude remember?"

Ralph stood up looking decidedly woozy. He held on to the armchair for support. "I don't believe you. You know her. Your old man knew her. Dad, the randy old bastard sure did."

Provoked beyond measure Jude moved in on the other man, for all Ralph's bulk, spinning him around to face him. "I've never laid eyes on Ms Costello until today," he said in a don't-mess-with-me voice. "Nor she on me. My father never ever mentioned her name. I've told you before to leave my father out of it. He was an honourable man.''

"Okay. Okay.'' Ralph tried to break Jude's grip. Gave up. "This whole thing is bizarre.''

"I agree.'' Jude took his time removing his hand, though his body language didn't change. There was a chance Ralph would swing the moment he turned his back.

"I want you to leave,'' Cate repeated, still looking white and wary. "I don't want you to ever come back. If you do I will report you to the police. If I have to I'll take out a restraining order. I don't know what you want with me, but I want absolutely nothing of you.''

Ralph struck his forehead as though trying to clear his brain. "You'd better talk to her, Conroy. I don't know what game she's playin'.'' All the fight seemed to have drained out of him. He looked sick.

Cate's green eyes flicked to Jude. "Game?''

She was doing a marvellous job of playing the innocent. "What else could it possibly be?'' Jude found himself saying in a cynical voice.

"Yeah, get it out of her, Jude.'' Ralph took the opportunity to lumber to the door, where he steadied himself with one long arm pressed against the jamb. "You damned well knew why I came, girl. You're no fool. No sirree! You're one exotic little chick, I've never seen any girl look like you. Dad must have had himself one hell of a good time.''

The girl looked quickly at Jude, her expression stunned. "What's he raving about? Do you know?''

For a second Jude almost believed her. As an actress she'd get a standing ovation. "I'm quite sure you know the truth, Ms Costello. You know the reason I'm here in town. You must have a good idea why Ralph decided to visit you, and you can count yourself lucky I arrived when I did.''

"Well, I'll try to!'' she told him sharply, greatly upset

by his demeanour. Everything about him—his eyes, his expression, his body language—told her for whatever reason Jude Conroy had now concluded he didn't like or trust her. What had happened since their last meeting to cause this hostility? "If it comes to that, I don't know why you're here, either?" She showed him an angry, spirited face.

"If you have the time I'll tell you," he shot back.

"That's it, Jude. Call her bluff," Ralph counselled, starting to move onto the timber deck. "She's probably on the game. I'll leave you to it. Just make sure your trip up here hasn't been a waste of time."

Jude watched him lurch away. Spoke up. "You're drunk, Ralph. You shouldn't be driving your car."

Ralph waved a contemptuous hand. "Don't tell me what to do, pal, and don't try to stop me. I've been drivin' for a very long time. The cops don't worry me, either."

"Let's hope they get you." Bolstered by Jude's presence and his palpable air of command, Cate walked to the door and slammed it on Ralph. She was trembling now that it was all over. Or was it? She realised Jude had become antagonistic towards her but for all her problems she found it difficult not to trust him. That was an awfully big step for her had he known it. He'd been furious with Rogan and he couldn't hide that from her. Furious and disgusted, ready to get into a fight. The tension in his naturally graceful body was obvious, small wonder Rogan had backed off.

"Thank goodness he's gone!" She tried to sound calm when she wasn't. She was shaking badly, trembling with outrage.

"You realise he could have harmed you?" Jude was still angry with her, but concerned by what he was seeing. Even given the natural creaminess of her skin she was very pale. Her beautiful eyes were like saucers.

"It did occur to me," she offered shortly. She wasn't

about to tell him the hidden places in her life. "He certainly changed his tune with you."

"Ralph and I go back a long way," he said, his complex feelings swallowed up by a larger concern. "I think I'll make you some tea, if you'll point me in the right direction."

Cate sat down before her legs gave way. "Tea's fine. Milk, one sugar. Sugar in the small yellow canister on the counter, tea in the medium-size one, milk in the frig."

"I ought to check he's gone," Jude said. It seemed possible Ralph might hang about. "Won't be a moment."

He was quick. Cate closed her eyes briefly in an effort to pull herself together. When she reopened them he was back through the door.

"The car's gone. Useless to try to stop him short of knocking him senseless." Despite himself he was touched by her delicacy, the vulnerable quiver in her limbs. Everything about her unsettled him. "He's going to kill himself one day."

"As long as it's no one else." Cate watched him move to the kitchen, deftly going about his self imposed job. The elegance of movement was made more apparent by his height. He found the cups and saucers first go. "So what's the mystery?" she asked. "Why exactly did he come here? Why was he calling me vile names? It wouldn't be difficult to persuade me he's quite mad."

"Maybe he is a touch," Jude said. "You can't think why he came?" He looked across at her, blue eyes probing.

"I think you'd better tell me." She turned her arm to examine a blue bruise.

"Brute!" Jude gritted when he saw it.

"I bruise easily."

"We can talk as soon as you get this tea into you. I've taken the liberty of adding a bit more sugar."

"Oh, dear! I hate it sweet."

"Trust me, you've had a bad fright." It was one she might have foreseen, he thought. The tea brewed, he poured two cups and put one in front of her. "Drink up."

"Later." She was still watching him with a puzzled look.

"No, now. You're very pale. In fact you look to me like you're in shock."

She shrugged. "What woman wouldn't be confronted by that gorilla?" She picked up the cup, embarrassed when her hand shook so badly she spilt a little.

"Did that burn you?" Naturally solicitous Jude moved away to fetch a paper towel. "Give me that." He took the cup from her, setting it down on the coffee table. "Ralph enjoys being mean to women, he's not so crash hot with us guys."

"I'm amazed he hasn't gone to jail." She dipped her head, feeling foolishly nerve ridden.

"Maybe too many women let him off the hook. You could have called the police. Bill Bennett is a good man."

"I realise that."

He felt his old protective streak rising. "A nip of brandy wouldn't go astray. Have you any?"

"No. I'm okay." Cate made a much better attempt at picking up her cup, willing the tremble out of her hand. She sipped at the hot tea, pulled a little involuntary face at the excessive sweetness. "I'm new here. The gallery is important to me. I have to succeed."

His blue gaze that had been kind and concerned, reverted to cynical. "You appear to have succeeded nicely."

"How would you know that?" She contrived to look as innocent as a child. "You haven't seen the gallery?"

"Just let's sit quietly for a moment." She appeared nearly exhausted. It made him frown and rub his chin. One moment she showed fierce defiance the next extreme vulnerability, it must be all part of her reaction to the shock.

Obediently Cate swallowed the rest of the tea in the cup, set it down. "You're being very considerate for a man who's decided he doesn't much like me."

He gave an abrupt laugh. "I haven't made any decision until I sort this thing out."

"What thing? You're in town as the Rogan lawyer?"

Jude raised an eyebrow. "Hey, so you've figured that out?"

"The truth is I'm quite smart, or smart enough. Your father was the town lawyer and I know you work for a top legal firm in Brisbane. It's quite amazing how often you and your father figure in the conversations around here."

"So I imagine you've heard about my mother?" There was the barest suggestion of bitterness in his voice though he tried hard to keep it out.

She hesitated, afraid she might say the wrong thing. She knew all about the walking wounded. "I've heard she was very beautiful and well liked. I heard you and your father were broken-hearted when she left."

"What would you expect?"

"Nothing less. I'm sorry." She spoke haltingly, but sincerely.

The sympathy in her green eyes disconcerted him. "It's all in the past," he said crisply. "Are you able to tell me now why you were at the funeral? You admitted you didn't know the family."

"I didn't realise I had to confide in you," she retorted, the ready sympathy dissolving at his tone. "You're a lawyer. You might have charged me with something for all I know. The fact is I don't know Lester Rogan's family."

"But you knew Lester?" He studied her closely. The colour was coming back into her cheeks. "You had a friendship. An intimacy?"

She looked angry and confused. "He was my landlord, you call that being intimate? The closest I ever came to intimacy was passing over the rent."

"Which he collected personally?" Jude asked in a purring voice.

"Can't you sit down?" She stared at him, admiring and not wanting to, the elegant way his lean body lounged back against the bench. "I don't like you towering over me."

"Sorry!" The distinctive dimple flicked in and out. "I thought I was keeping my distance. I'll take a chair." He moved to the two-seater sofa opposite her. "You were saying about the rent?"

"Do you want to check if it was too high or too low?"

"Nothing like that. Only if he collected it personally."

"Well, he did." Her answer was brisk. "Every fortnight."

"Fancy that! A busy man like Lester Rogan, a property tycoon no less, took time off every fortnight to call on you for the rent. Didn't you think that a little odd?"

"Actually I did," she admitted, "but who was I to argue? He was the landlord and he seemed to like coming in."

"Why not?" He gave her an enigmatic half smile. "So Tony sold out to him?"

"Don't take it personally."

He looked at her for a while, his expression a mix of amusement and cool speculation. "Did you talk much?"

"Well, yes, we did." She shrugged a shoulder. Her skin was as smooth as satin, the bones light and delicate. "He was a very interesting man. He wanted to know all about the crystals. Rather like you. How it all started. Not surprisingly he wanted to know something of my background."

"He managed to get that out of you?" The sarcasm escaped.

Her heart sped up. "You're barking up the wrong tree if you think he was trying to hit on me, Jude Conroy. He most definitely wasn't. He was rather sweet if you want to know. Gentlemanly."

Jude couldn't help it, he groaned in utter disbelief. "Of all the adjectives I could have lavished on the late Lester Rogan, sweet and gentlemanly wouldn't begin to figure. Lester had a wife but he preferred to have fun with other women. Everyone in town knows that."

She could feel the hot anger burgeoning in her. "I could think of a few adjectives for you. One isn't subtle. So what's bothering you exactly? Dare we take it to the hypothetical level? Even if I were mixed up with Lester Rogan— Why are you so angry?"

He met her eyes calmly, though it required an effort. Why indeed? "Maybe because I'm executor of his estate." That seemed reasonable enough.

"What's that got to do with me?" Her eyes opened wide, clear as crystal, windows of the soul.

"Oh, I can't stand another moment of this!" Jude sprang to his feet, pacing the area between kitchen and living room. The back wall was lined with bookcases crammed with books. Ms Costello was a reader it seemed. She also had a flair for interior decoration now that he thought about it. But it was as an actress that she took his breath away.

"Maybe you're allowing your imagination to run away with you?" she challenged. "Instead of pacing around my living room why don't you tell me what this is all about?"

"Try this." Jude resumed his seat opposite her, pinning her eyes. "I do hope you're ready. At least you're sitting down. It's my job to inform you, you figure largely in the late Lester Rogan's will. In fact he has left you the bulk of his estate. The big question looming in the family's mind is why? Would you have any idea? We're all striving to get the clear picture. Who are you, Ms Costello? I'm not trying to insult you, I really need to know.''

She'd been sitting with one slender leg curled beneath her, now she sat up straight lowering her narrow foot to the floor. ''Hang on a minute.'' She held up a hand. ''I'm trying to take in what you've just said.''

''You weren't prepared?'' It came out with more cynicism than he intended to show. ''Lester didn't drop any little hints?''

It cost her a considerable effort not to throw something at him. She hated the contempt in his eyes, the arrogant tilt of his blond head. ''Listen, I've had the most hideous experience with the dreadful Ralph, why do I have to listen to your taunts?''

His mouth compressed. ''I'd have thought because I'm the bearer of glad tidings. You've been left a fortune, Ms Costello, many millions in property and shares. You didn't know you were an heiress?''

Cate with the redhead's hot temper, sprang to her feet. ''Heiress? Listen, I'm about to freak out. If you're being absolutely serious and you're not drunk like your friend—''

''Friend?'' Jude grimaced. ''I resent that. I'm stone cold sober and Ralph Rogan was never my friend. If you've a Bible in the house I'll swear on it. It's just as I said. the late Lester Rogan has bequeathed to you the bulk of his fortune.''

''I don't believe it.'' Shocked and baffled she stared at him, trying to absorb such sensational news.

''I do actually,'' he told her dryly. Green eyes glowing. White skin. Bright copper hair raining down her back. It was all too easy to believe. ''I'll read it all out to you. Just say the word. Is there the remote possibility you're his love child?''

"Come on please!" Cate shuddered, turning away in agitation. "You think I'd want to be related to the goon that came here?"

"Strangely enough Ralph can look good at times…he has no difficulty attracting women. He was drunk. Some might find that understandable given the fact he'd sustained a horrendous shock. I know it's unfair, but we can't pick our brothers and sisters."

"You're having fun aren't you?" she accused him with quiet disgust.

Actually he was having a great deal of trouble taking his eyes off her. He'd never seen a girl look better in a skimpy pair of shorts "I assure you I'm not. This is a very serious matter. I can see the family trying to prove Lester was in the last stages of dementia."

"He must have been." Cate put a hand against her head. "This is a terrible mistake."

"The Rogans certainly think so," he offered suavely.

"Obviously you agree." She was confused and disturbed by the changes in him. When they'd met after the funeral he'd been someone else entirely. Smiling into her eyes, charming, sexy. Very, very sexy. Someone who'd attracted her powerfully. Now the atmosphere between them was electric with distrust.

His very next words confirmed it. "I can't think you're being honest with me," he said.

"Oh, I've got that." She shrugged. "Are legal men always so suspicious?"

"I'm afraid so. It goes with the territory. Lester Rogan had to have very good reason to make you his main beneficiary. He had to feel very strongly about you."

"There's a problem there. He forgot to tell me. In fact

he was nothing more than pleasant every time I saw him. Didn't the family get anything? Surely not?'' She stared at him, hurt by his attitude even if she half understood it. It didn't look good for her. ''No wonder the son came after me. He was beside himself with rage.''

''You risked a fate worst than death opening that door,'' Jude clipped off, his expression darkening. ''You asked a question. I'll answer it. Mrs Rogan, her daughter, Melinda and her son Ralph who took it upon himself to make your acquaintance this evening, all received a considerable bequest. It should keep them happily for the rest of their days if they listen to their advisers.''

''Isn't that you?'' she abruptly challenged, picking up a lemon from a basket as though she intended to throw it at him. Instead she only held it in her palm, then put it back in the basket. ''Did you benefit by the way?'' This time she turned the sarcasm on him.

He kept his expression dispassionate. ''Why ever would you ask that question?''

''Why ever not?'' she countered. ''Surely it was part of your studies learning to keep a straight face? You do it well. Everyone knows lawyers benefit handsomely from clients' wills, we read about it all the time in the papers. Sometimes the family get angry about it and take action.''

''Which may well happen to you,'' he pointed out.

''I don't want the money.'' She shook back her long copper hair.

''You might well say that now.'' His expression was sardonic.

''I happen to mean it.''

''Well, you could give it away,'' he suggested lightly. ''Rehabilitation centres, charities, your friends, young people on the dole, pensioners. There's no shortage of deserving people who need the money.''

"Sarcasm is sweet on your tongue. But this is crazy!"

"Of course it is," he agreed, frowning in thought. "So crazy I don't feel like leaving you here on your own."

She stared out at the deck. "You think Godzilla might return?"

She spoke with bravado, but there was something going on behind her green eyes. Jude studied her, trying to figure out what it was. "I have to tell you I have concerns. You need more security around this place if you're going to live here."

"Why would I live here?" She threw up her slender arms looking like a beautiful witch about to launch into an incantation. "Haven't I come into a fortune? I have to face it. I'm an heiress. Isn't that what you just said." She stared back at him, bright flags of colour in her cheeks.

"Ralph never figured on the estate being broken up the way it has been," he answered soberly. "He expected the bulk of it to pass to him by divine right. I have to confess I expected it. You can bet your life the whole town expected it. Of course I can see what the town might think is neither here nor there to you anymore. If you continued to live here, however, everyone would consider they had the right to hear why Lester Rogan did what he did."

"Why don't you look into it?" she challenged, taking a step toward him. "You're the successful lawyer. Precisely how much do you charge an hour?"

"Quite a lot," he said dryly, "but you could afford it now."

She gave a little half laugh with no humour in it. "I'm not afraid to stay here, I'll be quite safe." Inside she was quivering like a plucked string. Ralph Rogan's aggression tapped in to too many old nightmares.

He could see straight through the pretence. "You'll be a lot safer with me. You really should have a good security door fitted. I'm surprised you haven't. And get locks on the windows—this place would be a piece of cake to get into.''

As though she didn't know. ''No one has bothered me up to now. I'm just a bit strung up at the moment.''

A strained pause followed. Jude broke it. ''I'm amazed no one has bothered you looking like you do. I would have thought you'd be fighting off callers? Either that, or everyone thought—''

''Thought what?'' She lifted her chin, daring him to say it.

''Callers were likely to make Lester angry,'' he said finally. ''If you thought Ralph intimidating Lester took good care not to show you his dark side. Why did you go to the funeral? Why did you cover your hair so you wouldn't stand out? That says a lot. You must have cared about the man. You're holding back plenty and I know it.''

She caught the wave of hostility, took a deep breath. ''I went to pay my respects. I wasn't alone. There was a crowd.''

He nodded. ''Yes, small. Lester made a lot of enemies around here. A lot of people thought making enemies was the sort of thing he liked to do. Not you. You knew him as sweet and gentlemanly. Obviously he was heavily camouflaged or you're not being truthful. Whatever you tell me will be treated in confidence.''

Anger consumed her. ''There's nothing to tell,'' she said sharply. ''My friendship with Mr Rogan can be examined by the whole world for all I care. It was perfectly respectable. He was not my father in case you're thinking of following up that line.''

His face tautened. ''I need your help, Ms Costello. Would you mind telling me about your parents.''

''I do mind actually.'' She knew she sounded as defensive as she felt. She couldn't control it. ''If there had been any connection with Lester Rogan I'd have known about it. I need to think about this. It really is a tremendous shock whatever you may think.''

Tension was showing in her face and her body language, it was mirrored in her beautiful eyes. He stood up, stunned by the way she got to him and his deep dormant emotions. ''We can go over the will any time that suits. I'm having lunch with an old friend of my father's, tomorrow, otherwise I'm free. I'm not happy about leaving you here, I have a house at Spirit Cove, it's the family home, there's plenty of room and you could stay the night. Then I'd know you were safe.''

She felt so jittery she was tempted. ''That's okay. I'll sleep like a baby.''

''I very much doubt that!'' He turned back, his eyes running over her. ''I won't sleep thinking of you here,'' he admitted frankly, aware his own nerves were on edge. What was to stop Ralph from doubling back? ''Why don't you shove a few things in a bag and come with me.''

She swallowed on the hard knot in her throat. Whether he disliked her or not she could see his genuine concern. ''I prefer to stay here.'' She moved away, her movements brittle, a little helpless.

''No, you don't,'' he said firmly. ''I'm involved now. I know how to handle it. You've had a bad fright, I can see it in your eyes. Frankly I consider it a miracle I got here when I did. I don't want to worry you unnecessarily, but Ralph could be anywhere out there waiting for me to go.''

She was very much afraid of that, yet she argued: ''What's to stop him coming back any other night? Day for that matter?''

Jude's eyes raced over her. Her beauty was attacking all his senses. He found those little gestures of her hands strangely moving. She'd be irresistible to any man. He felt desperate to be convinced the late Lester Rogan hadn't been one of them. "I'm going to read Ralph the riot act when he's sober. I think I can put the fear of God into him for a while until we sort this thing out."

CHAPTER FOUR

WHILE she packed a few things, Jude went around the flat checking on windows and doors, not that anyone couldn't have broken in if they wanted to, but Isis was a peaceful, law-abiding town where people still continued to go out and leave their back doors unlocked. He wouldn't advise it, however, for a beautiful young woman living on her own. She needed the proper protection.

She hadn't told him about her connection to Tony Mandel either, or what she was doing in such a back-water, albeit tropical paradise. It baffled him to think she had chosen to live and work in a small coastal town. Most young people headed off to the cities to find work and excitement, returning years later when it was time to opt out of the rat race. His father, a clever man who could have done a lot better for himself career-wise had never wished to live anywhere else. Unlike Jude who couldn't get out quick enough to embark upon his career.

At twenty-eight he was on the fast track, considered pretty damned good, but amazingly he wasn't all that happy. He had Poppy Gooding to worry about for one thing. She threatened to jeopardize his job. He'd never felt more like taking a break, but instead he'd been dished up a dilemma.

"All set?"

"Yes." She came back into the living room, carrying a small overnight bag. She had changed the white shorts for a long sarong type skirt printed in big open-faced hibiscus, pretty blue sandals on her feet. He felt like reaching for her but that would never do.

"I'll take that," he said, putting out his hand for her bag.

"Thank you. Do you think I should leave a light or two on?"

He shook his head. "It won't make a difference if you turn them off. I've checked the windows."

"Anyone could get in," she said in a fatalistic kind of voice, starting to switch off lights. "Tony didn't care. He didn't worry about a thing."

"Tony was a man well able to take care of himself. I don't believe in women going short on security measures." He wanted to ask her about Tony but left it until they were in the car speeding away to Spirit Cove. There was no sign of a red sports car anywhere.

"So how did you meet Tony?" he decided to broach the subject. He realised he knew absolutely nothing about her which made his response to her all the more breathtaking. Her profile was as cleanly cut as a cameo, her skin luminous even in the low light reflected off the dashboard.

"It's a long story. I don't think I can tell you tonight."

"Okay. Tony never mentioned anyone like you and I've known him most of my life."

"He's a good friend, a good man," she said softly.

"Yes, he is."

"He painted me."

That piece of information given so simply startled him. "Now why isn't that a surprise?"

He had one of those voices capable of infinite nuances, Cate thought. At the moment, light sarcasm, a touch of self-mockery. She wondered how she'd found it so easy to come with him when she'd been near assaulted, her every sensibility mangled. It was as though Jude Conroy with his beautiful smile had breeched her every defence. It was odd for someone like her who had lived through dark traumas and kept silent about them for years.

"Tony had a special affinity with beautiful things," he was saying, his tone revealing his affection for his father's friend. "Beautiful women, beautiful flowers, beautiful birds, beautiful tropical sunsets. Where's the portrait now?"

"It's at the gallery."

"On show?" He gave her another quick sidelong glance.

"No. It's in my bedroom."

"I'd like to see it."

He said it in no way suggestively, it sounded as though he were just interested. "You can sometime," she promised.

"Big? Small?" he questioned. "Either way it'd be valuable. At home and abroad. Tony is making quite a name for himself."

"It's a big painting actually. A lovely painting. The treatment of light and colour is wonderful."

Jude was thoroughly intrigued. Of course Tony wouldn't have been able to resist her as a model just as he hadn't been able to resist Jude's mother who had also been Tony's model. Cate Costello was not only beautiful she had so much more to her—the obvious intelligence, plus a bewitching quality that was playing havoc with all the defence mechanisms he had in place. "So when did he paint it? Before he went overseas?"

"A long time before that, I was twelve going on thirteen at the time." There was wistfulness, nostalgia in her voice. She'd been a child in a beautiful garden setting shimmering with light—banks of white azaleas behind her—staring out of the glowing canvas with big green eyes. She'd been red-blond then, her skin very white. Later her hair had deepened to its present bright copper.

Jude was battling all the surprises that were coming thick and fast. Her past seemed strewn with secrets. "So you've known Tony for years? What are you now, twenty-two?"

"Twenty-three my next birthday. Do you believe in fate, Jude?"

Even the sound of his name on her lips unsettled him. It sounded so silky—tender. "Yes, I do."

"Tony was a friend of my mother's. He's been a good friend to me."

"And your mother?" He glanced at her quickly. "You used the past tense."

A soft cry broke from her. Pure pain. A full moment of silence, then: "My mother...disappeared," she told him in a near inaudible voice, as though she couldn't endure to let the words pass her lips. "She's never been found."

Jude was utterly stunned. He was upset his question had been so clumsy. Great misery surrounded that heart-wrenching disclosure. "I'm so sorry, Cate. How dreadful for you."

"Beyond dreadful," she said. "A torture."

"I can imagine." The loss of his own mother approached that. "Her name was Costello?" he asked gently, wracking his brains to recall a story on a missing woman called Costello.

"No." She shook her head. "My mother remarried a couple of years after my father was killed in a car smash when I was ten. I loved him very much. He was so full of love and life and energy."

"How have you managed to rise above all this pain?" He wished it was light enough to see her expression. He was struck by the fact, her life like his, had been shattered by conflict and tragedy.

Her head averted she stared out the window. The stars over the ocean were thickly clustered; infinite acres of diamond daisies. "I'm an orphan like you only the chances of your mother still being alive are good. Do you never want to see her, Jude?"

He hesitated as though unsure what he could admit to. Finally he said, too harshly, "I can't let my mother back into my heart or my life again."

"That sounds very final." She winced at the bitter note of rejection even though she knew there was grief and suffering too.

He was quiet for a moment. "It is."

"I'd give anything just to know my mother was alive," Cate said. "To see her one more time." Her voice conveyed a wealth of emotion.

"And she disappeared just like that?" Jude looked directly at her. "There was a search of course?" There had to be…no one just disappeared.

She nodded. "Nationwide. My mother married a man called Carl Lundberg."

The name swam out of his subconscious. "Lundberg. I remember now." The case had attracted a lot of notoriety. Professor Lundberg was an eminent academic, wealthy in his own right, highly respected in the community. It had to be six or seven years back. Mrs Lundberg—she'd been much younger than her husband—had last been seen setting off with the family dog, a collie, on a walk through the national forest reserve adjacent to the Lundberg's large colonial home. Neither she nor the family dog had been seen again.

"It was as though my mother and our dog, Blaze, disappeared off the face of the earth," she said, sounding so lost and mournful he caught at her hand in an effort to comfort.

"I'm so sorry, Cate. Why does so much tragedy come into certain peoples' lives and bypass others? The only route to survival seems to be to accept. I remember it was a very baffling case. The file won't have been closed. The police never give up."

She nodded. "They were very kind to me but sometimes it's almost impossible to find enough evidence to lay charges. I believe he killed her."

Jude's heart rocked. He dared not speak for several fraught moments. "Why would you believe that?" he asked finally, keeping his tone very calm. "The investigation would have been very thorough. The husband is always a prime suspect. You must have been around sixteen?"

"He did it," she repeated. "Heaven knows why I'm telling you all this, you're the first person I've spoken to about it in years. He had an alibi of sorts—he claimed to have been at the university all day. He was seen by staff and students on and off and there was never enough to arrest him. Why would anyone suspect such a distinguished man? He had, still has, so many important friends and supporters.

"He acted as though his own life had come to an end. He played the distraught husband to the hilt. I was the jealous, paranoid, difficult daughter that he'd tried so hard to win over but never succeeded. I wouldn't allow him to take my father's place, he said. That was certainly true." She gave a brittle laugh. "As though a man like that, a man in a mask, ever could. At the end of the day the police had nothing against him. I can't blame them for my rush to judgment. I was such a mess."

"I'm not surprised," he said grimly. "What you're saying is appalling. Obviously with your loss a terrible resentment towards your stepfather held sway, but have you never considered during these intervening years you could have been mistaken?"

"I'm not mistaken," Cate said through gritted teeth. "I hate him. If my mother had never met him she'd still be alive."

They were approaching the house. Both of them had fallen silent, both struck dumb. Jude was utterly pole-axed by what he had learned. How could he possibly have fore-seen this dramatic turn of events? He'd thought it would be all routine; finalising Rogan's will, then taking a quiet vacation at home. That day dream had been blasted away.

There was so much he had to find out about the beautiful, mysterious creature beside him. There was too much he didn't understand. Why she had moved to this particular town, so far off the beaten track? What was the mother's connection to Tony Mandel? At the top of the list, what was Cate's connection to her benefactor? In view of what she had told him he now found it impossible to believe she had deliberately drawn Lester Rogan into her net though the possibility remained her mother could have bewitched Lester. Was it possible she was Lester's natural daughter and Lester found out years later? Jude had learned enough about life to know just getting through it was a very bumpy ride.

He'd left lights burning. They moved into the house, he standing back so she could proceed him. Now that he had her here he felt fractionally easier. The house was so peaceful, so welcoming with the shade of his father about.

She paused a moment in the entrance hall, with its bright rug and golden polished floor, looking about her. "This is a lovely old house," she said gently. "I love tropical architecture. I've seen the house from the road many times and admired it. I like going for drives Sunday afternoon, looking at the local houses and the pole houses at the beach. I much prefer this to the Rogan mansion. Glorious views, but I don't care for the residence."

She moved into the living room where one of Tony Mandel's magnificent bird paintings hung above the white painted mantle. The painting, one of a number bought by his father, was of a group of white jabirus, the tall Australian storks, with black tails and bills standing out in contrast to a turquoise-blue lagoon, a deeper blue sky with a trail of white clouds and lush tropical vegetation.

Jude turned on more lights to improve her viewing. That afternoon he'd slashed a dozen flower bracts of the very showy Red Ginger that grew in abundance in the garden, shoving them into a tall glass vase and placing them on the low coffee table as a splash of colour. His mother had always brought lots of flowers into the house. She'd been an expert at arrangements; wonderful imaginative showpieces that utilized a lot of big tropical leaves.

"You must have picked these," Cate said, touching a scarlet sprout. She liked the idea of his wanting to have flowers in the house.

He shrugged, suddenly consumed by inexpressible feelings. "I did my fair share of gardening when I was a kid. There was a time my parents were passionate about their garden."

"It's still a beautiful garden," she said. "Tony's painting looks marvellous up there. He gets a surreal quality into his work."

Jude nodded. "There are others scattered through the house." He didn't know why he added it but he did. "He painted my mother, too. Tony couldn't resist a beautiful woman."

She turned to stare at him, her copper head tilted a little to the side. "Do you still have it or did your mother—"

"Take it with her?" he interrupted more bitterly than he intended. A dead give-away. "She walked out with just the clothes on her back and never returned. The guy she went off with was a rich American. He could afford her."

She looked back at the arrangement of Red Ginger. "How very sad for your father and you. Where's the portrait now?"

"It's on the next floor. Dad did take it down, but evidently he put it back up. Looks like he never could stop loving her. You want to see it?''

"If that doesn't upset you?" For all his controlled demeanour she could see it would be a test.

"Come up. I'll take your overnight bag. The bedrooms are upstairs. It won't take a few minutes to make up the bed in the guest room. An old pal of my Dad's keeps the house aired and the grounds tidy."

"Jimmy Dawson?" she smiled.

"Do you know Jimmy?" In the act of picking up her bag, he set it down again to stare at her.

"How wouldn't I get to know Jimmy? He's one of the local characters. He often pops in for a "yarn" or to bring me something of interest. He used to be a prospector, travelled all over the Outback. He's got opals, sapphires, garnets, carnelians and topaz. He has quite a collection of agates, too, chrysoprase—Chrysoprase is a translucent apple-green stone he says reminds him of my eyes."

"A ladies' man is Jimmy," he commented dryly.

"Aren't they all?" she answered brightly enough, then appeared engulfed by unhappy thoughts.

"Come up," he repeated, to distract her, leading the way.

The same mahogany stair tread creaked as they walked up. Her hand clung lovingly to the beautiful carved banister.

The portrait of his mother held pride of place. It dominated the space at the end of the wide corridor. His father's bedroom, the main bedroom his parents had shared, gave directly off it. He'd kept to the bedroom of his boyhood at the other end of the house. There were four double bedrooms with en suite in all. The bedroom he had in mind for her was midway along the corridor.

Jude paused outside it to put down her overnight bag and turn on the light. Cate continued to walk compulsively towards the portrait of Sally Conroy. What she saw was a beautiful sexual woman revealed in her prime. There was no mistaking Jude's resemblance to his mother. The thick curly golden hair, the dazzling blue eyes that drew you in. Sally was smiling, not a big smile more enigmatic, the familiar dimple etched into her cheek. That smile, like her son's, had great power. Cate was lost in admiration thinking Tony must have been a little in love with this woman. The painting seemed brim full of it. Love. Sensuality. Sally was wearing a rose-pink blouse that tumbled off her creamy shoulders and dipped low over lovely full breasts. Quite a woman!

Jude came up quietly behind her. "I'm thinking now Tony must have been in love with her. The whole thing has a voluptuous quality. Or that was my mother."

"You're extraordinarily like her."

"In looks maybe." He answered in a clipped voice. "Let me show you your room. There's a choice if you're not happy with this one, but I think it's the nicer." He stood back while she walked in.

"You're being very chivalrous, Jude." Involuntary tears came to her eyes. She walked across the large room to the French doors giving her the opportunity to blink them away. She knew Jude Conroy's feelings towards her were highly ambiguous, yet he was concerned for her welfare.

"That's me," he said laconically, moving to open the glass doors. Jimmy had already fastened all the green shutters back when he was airing the house. "This has a good view of the beach. I might have to get rid of a couple of pandanus. They've grown huge." He walked out onto the verandah and she followed him, both of them taking in long draught of the fresh salt air.

"It's paradise in the tropics!" she murmured." No wonder Tony spent so many years north of Capricorn painting."

"What's Tony to you?" he found himself asking, leaning

his hands on the white painted balustrade and staring out into the perfumed night.

A broken-hearted sadness swept over her. Would she ever be free of it? "Tony loved my mother. He said he should have married her only my father came along to ruin his chances. It wasn't destined. Tony was destined to become famous. My father was destined to die. My stepfather—" She broke off, abruptly changing the subject. "The air's like silk! Oh, look!" She pointed, voice rising." There's someone on the beach. Where did she come from?"

Jude stared hard into the semidarkness. "I don't see a thing." For a surreal second he imagined he did.

"You must!" Her voice had a little throb of urgency in it. "Out there, look. A woman. Her long skirt is blowing in the breeze."

All right, a game then! "There's no one there, Cate," he said, revealing his scepticism. "You've heard the story, that's all."

"Story?" She turned an inquiring face to him, innocent green eyes, enormous, jewel-like.

"About Spirit Cove's resident ghost." He let his sceptical gaze rest on her. She could have been an angel sent from Heaven only he knew better. She was far more the white-skinned temptress.

"That's no ghost," she protested indignantly. "That's a woman walking on the beach. You don't believe me?"

"'Fraid not." He shook his head.

"Then let's take a look," she challenged. "She couldn't have gone far. Come on. Don't stand there all glinty eyed like I've made her up."

To his astonishment she turned away in a flurry of long hair like apricot silk. She was running down the corridor, down the staircase, making instinctively for the back door.

"Cate!" He caught her up, shaking his head. "I don't believe this!"

"I've got to see her."

He watched her unlock the door, then she was tearing away into the night, so fleet of foot he didn't even have time to grab her hand.

"Cate, Cate, calm down." He had no recourse but to follow her, his eyes adjusting quickly to the gloom. He had to pause to turn on a few more exterior lights in case both of them broke their necks. By the time he reached the picket gate, she was no more than a streak on the sandy path that led to the beach. She could move. He'd say that for her, but the dunes were laced with grasses that hooked into the sand like a trap. Some kind of alarm was in him and he realised, a dangerous excitement that was building every moment he was with her. No way could he allow it to get the better of him. He had to be resolute!

The lights from the deck were almost gone now. She was lost in the starry darkness. He knew a few moments of pure panic. Hell, he was nearly losing his mind over her.

"Cate," he yelled, tough as nails. "Come back here. Come on, Cate. I can't see a damned thing." There was no moon, only a billion stars crowding the black velvet sky.

Which way did she go? Left, or right? She'd been looking towards the right. He knew everyone who lived around here. Most of the residents of the Cove were retirees, getting on in years. They did their walking early morning and late afternoon. He headed off towards the right, the sand pouring into his Nikes. Now he could make out her slender shape.

"Cate, I'd be real pleased if you didn't do things like this," he shouted. It was a wonder she didn't jump into the surf. Why the heck did she have to be so fascinating? It made everything so much more difficult. He daren't let anything happen. Imagine that face on his pillow! That sweet slender body beside him! She was just crying out to be made love to. He had to force himself to remember he was supposed to be the level-headed lawyer with duties to discharge.

She was moving so fast back along the beach she near stumbled right into his arms. "I'm telling you she was there," she gasped, her breath sweet on his cheek. "It's impossible that I imagined her."

He steadied her by holding her shoulders. A big mistake. Her skin was the softest, the silkiest he had ever touched. "Don't worry. It was nothing. I'll take you back."

She stared up at him. Though she actually couldn't see the expression on his face, it was too dark, she felt keenly aware he thought the whole thing might have been a stunt. "Jude, I saw her quite distinctly, that's why I followed her. She was wearing a long white dress."

"Even if you'd run faster you'd never have caught her up," he said wryly. Spirit Cove's ghost had been dead for over sixty years. He found himself putting an arm around her shoulders, excusing it as humouring her. He began to steer her back towards the house. Desire for her was mounting so hot and rapid he truly believed his ingrained caution might be thrown to the winds unless they moved off the beach. This minute. Night alone had special power. People didn't behave quite the same in the dark.

She was still protesting, anxious for him to believe her. "I tell you her long skirt was flapping in the breeze."

"Sure it wasn't a trick of the eye?" He wasn't about to tell her his own mother claimed to have seen a woman dressed in white walking along the beach at night. It wasn't long after that his mother left. He remembered now part of the myth was that the ghost was only seen by those at a crossroads in their lives.

"It was a real woman, Jude." She lifted her head in an

appealing gesture. "She must have gone up the dunes to one of the houses."

"She wouldn't have had time," he considered, shaking his head. "Our house is fairly isolated as you can see. My neighbours are quite a distance either way. It had to be a trick of the eye, Cate, there was no woman. It could have been the sea mist." He wasn't about to get into any discussion on the paranormal.

"Okay." She expelled a long breath. "I can see I won't convince you. I don't want an argument." Nevertheless she promptly broke away, leaving him to run after her yet again. "You're a witch aren't you?" he called, half laughing, half off balance. "All right then, I'll race you to the house. You've got a good start."

She said not a word, but continued to sprint away making good going in the soft sand. She was almost at the white picket gate that closed off the house from the beach when she lost her footing as dune grasses wound themselves tightly around her ankle and held it fast. She went over onto the soft sand, lifting her arms and laughing delightedly.

He thought he'd never heard a sound so exquisitely seductive. "Get me out of this sand trap!" she yelled.

He closed the distance to where she lay. "That's it! No more races for the night. The things you expect of me!" At least they were within range of the lights from the house. They shone on the flowerlike purity of her skin and her long copper hair, the light garments that covered her. He reached down for her and she grasped his hand. He truly only intended to pull her to her feet but somehow he didn't stop until he had her locked in his arms.

It was stunning, but he was kissing her, kissing her. It went on for ages, her soft full lips opened erotically beneath his, the taste ambrosial. His hand somehow was resting high up, alongside her breast. He had only to move his fingers for his palm to cup its exquisite contours. How he wanted to. "Oh God!" he whispered into her mouth. He was losing the battle for control, his blood pounding hot and feverish.

Things were happening so fast he could scarcely follow. He only knew he didn't want to let her go. He couldn't get enough of her. If only he could lower her down onto the sand, pull off that little top, bend his head to her naked breasts. She was doing nothing to curb him. Her body was pressed hard against his, her arousal seemingly as intense as his own.

"Jude, please..." Yet she was holding on to him with both hands. Where was this going to end? In a bed? His tongue played with hers, their bodies thrusting, grinding, one against the other. He had a heart-stopping vision of her naked beside him except for the beautiful silver bracelet she wore around her wrist. The perfume of gardenias clung to her; clung to her clothes, her face, her skin, clung to him. He'd never experienced such a furore over a kiss.

Suddenly the whole sequence changed. She broke away panting, as though she suddenly realized it was very wrong of her to trust him. Both of them were breathing hard, as though they were having difficulty getting enough air into their lungs.

"I'm sorry." For a moment he couldn't think of another thing to say. "I'd no right to do that. The last thing I want to do is frighten you. Put it down to the night." He didn't put voice to his craving though she would have felt his rock hardness against her. He wanted to catch her back, make love to her until she moaned and didn't know whether to faint. He wanted to tell her about his scars, his sense of betrayal and rejection, his childhood baggage, above all. He knew with her own experiences of pain and despair she would understand.

Her answer was no more than a whisper. "It's all right, Jude. We're both off balance."

Off balance yes, but it was perfect. Kisses that made a man tremble. But then he'd wanted to kiss her since he'd first laid eyes on her in the little timber church. Imagine wanting someone so much at first sight! He was more than half in love with her yet he knew so little about her. It was even possible she wasn't as truly beautiful as she appeared to be. Allowing himself to fall further under her spell would be like jumping into a tropical lagoon with no thought of what might be lurking beneath the water.

Neither spoke a word until they were inside the house with the back door locked and the bolt shot.

"I'll go check on the bed linen," he said, giving them both a chance to calm down. "I haven't had much to eat, have you?"

With surprise she realized she was hungry, even ravenous. "I was thinking of preparing something when that appalling Ralph arrived. What have you got?"

"Nothing much." He shrugged, amazed he sounded normal. "We could have an omelette, toast, there's quite a bit of roast chicken left, bacon. Fresh garden herbs in a jar—I like the smell of them in the kitchen. Tea, coffee, a packet of shortbread biscuits. Jimmy left a few supplies but I have to do lots of shopping."

Wisely she didn't offer to help him make up the bed. "I'll whip up the omelettes. I just hope you've got the right pan. That's absolutely vital."

"I'm sure you'll find it," he called back as he mounted the stairs.

When he returned she had set the table in the family room, using the glass-topped wicker table surrounded by four comfortably upholstered chairs. She had found bright yellow place mats, cutlery, condiments, a couple of tulip shaped wineglasses. "I thought we might have a glass of the chardonnay, okay? Help me sleep."

"Sure. Want me to open the bottle?" He was pleased with himself he sounded so cool. She was so beautiful and he had palmed her breast.

"Please. The omelettes are ready." Cate was having difficulty controlling her own excitement. It was like a brilliant dancing light.

"So you found the right pan?" He located the wine opener, deftly uncorked the bottle.

"You have everything one could possibly need."

He just saved himself from saying his mother had been a great cook consequently she'd accumulated every bit of equipment a serious chef would need.

The wine was nicely chilled. He poured each of them a glass, passed hers to her. "Cheers!" He held up his glass in salute.

"Cheers!" she responded. "Take a seat."

He laughed, unaware of the vivid animation in his face. "You walk right into my house and start cooking."

"Hope you like it." She set a plate before him.

"Say this looks very professional!" He stared down at the fluffy concoction on his plate. His didn't turn out like this.

"I'm really good with omelettes." She turned to him with a smile. "Plenty of practice and help from recipe books. I love cookbooks, I love books period."

"So I saw back at the gallery."

"My father always encouraged me to read," she said almost dreamily. "He said very little about his early life but he did tell me once the house where he was born had a wonderful library."

She had his absolute attention. "How interesting! Revealing

as well. A house with a wonderful library probably was quite a house.''

"I suppose.'' From her expression she regretted having said anything at all. "I didn't have any parmesan so I grated your cheddar,'' she told him, briskly changing the subject. "I've used your chives as well and I'm afraid six of your eggs.''

"That okay. I'll go shopping tomorrow. This looks good.''

"Eat up before it goes cold.''

"You're going to join me?'' His eyes couldn't seem to let go of her.

"Of course.''

"Hasn't this been an unexpected night?'' He watched her moving around his kitchen as though it were her own. She looked back suddenly and caught him, the colour rising to her cheeks.

"It has indeed.'' She joined him at the table, bringing with her hot toast and curls of butter in a white bowl.

She'd worked fast. He was amazed how hungry he was. Amazed about everything. She was almost a total stranger yet he felt as though she'd always been in his life. That wasn't easy to understand. He allowed himself to toy with thoughts of a soul mate. Two wandering souls destined to be joined. Maybe there was something in it after all.

The omelette was so good. "Have you someone in your life, a boyfriend?'' he asked after a while. Hell, he hadn't planned on saying that. Why did he? Answer: because he desperately wanted to know.

She shook her head, put down her fork.

"I have no idea why I asked you that,'' he said.

"Particularly when you've half convinced yourself Lester Rogan was my sugar daddy.''

It was his turn to shake his head. "I can't believe you'd go in for that sort of thing."

"You don't want to believe?"

They exchanged a long glance. "I surely don't. Besides, you've got too much character and depth. And you're wounded. You've got a wounded heart."

"Takes one to know one, Jude," she said quietly.

They shared the bottle of wine and afterwards he made the coffee, the two of them moving of one accord onto the spacious deck. "I think I saw a ghost tonight," she confided, having arrived at her conclusion. "What's more I'm prepared to stick by it."

His low laugh made her tingle. "What are you trying to do? Frighten me to death?"

"I'm not afraid of ghosts," she said.

"I don't believe in them. I can't."

She studied him with those jewel-like eyes, the pupils extended tenderly. "That's not true, Jude. I'm sure you feel your father moving about the house? You feel him as a gentle presence. You smile to yourself when the tread creaks on the staircase."

He couldn't deny it. "How do you know that?"

"Maybe I have extrasensory perception. Maybe losing my mother so suddenly, so violently, is part of it."

"You're sure violence was done, Cate?" There were so many secrets to be drawn out of her.

"Yes, it seemed like a futureless future without my mother. I only pray it was fast." She focused on the floodlit garden with its abundant fruit trees.

"Listen to me, Cate." He reached for her hand. "It'll be all right."

She shook her head. "It'll never be all right."

"Was your stepfather a violent man?" That was not rare

even in a man of culture. He could have been the classic street angel, home devil Jude thought.

"That's what makes it so unreal." She couldn't keep calm with his thumb warm on her pulse. She made a pretence of wanting her coffee and he let her go. "He never laid a finger on her. There was no physical abuse but she came to fear him."

A strange feeling passed over Jude, like a surge of dread. "It sounds like you feared him, too. He must have been very controlling?"

In front of his eyes her whole body went rigid. "He was. Mum almost had to have his permission to go out the door." Her eyes glittered with tears she blinked fiercely away.

It was all he could do not to take her protectively into his arms. "I understand why you couldn't bear to live in the same house as him."

She lowered her head, biting her lip. "I never ever want to lay eyes on him again, but I know I will."

"Cate, one way or another it will come right." His words came like a solemn promise.

"Not in a thousand years!"

"I understand how you feel, but survival is dependant on acceptance, we both know that. Ultimately we have to move on. Are you absolutely sure your mother wasn't planning a new life somewhere? My father trusted my mother. So did I. Look what she did to us."

Cate nodded. "She failed you. I'm so sorry. But my mother would never have left without me." She cleared her long hair from the side of her face. "I was sixteen years old, I wasn't even finished high school. We loved one another. She has never touched her bank accounts nor used her credit card. In March of next year she'll be declared legally dead."

He could see she was broken-hearted. "You hated the man who replaced your father?" That happened, too.

"He never replaced him." Her expression changed to one of swift contempt. "He was charming to begin with—they always are—he entertained a lot. Everyone liked my mother. She was a wonderful hostess and so pretty."

"She would be if you resemble her."

"I don't," she murmured. "I'm my father's side of the family. I have the Costello colouring. Or so my father told me."

"You don't know your father's family?" he asked in surprise. "You've never had any contact?" That, too, was extraordinary but it happened.

She shook her head. "No. I think there must have been some trouble, some family rift. Besides, they're a long way away. Ireland. West of Ireland, I think. One day I'll find out, but so much has happened. My father came to Australia on his own, I know that. He was fresh out of university, an architect. He joined a firm in Sydney, although apparently he never saw eye to eye with them about anything. He went into private practice, but eventually he became a university lecturer. That's where my parents met Lundberg. It had to be the worst day of their lives."

"So what happened after your mother disappeared?" He stared at her intently. "Feeling as you did how did you continue to live with your stepfather?"

"I didn't." She shuddered. "Not even vacations. My mother had a close friend, Deborah, and she took control. She suggested to my stepfather it would be best if I boarded until I finished school. He was very much against it, but she managed to persuade him. I think she exerted some sort of pressure. She never liked him, either. After I finished school, I hit the road."

"Hit the road? Pardon me? What does that mean exactly?"

She looked back at him, a strange little smile hovering on her lips. "You surely don't think I was going to stay around even with Deborah to protect me."

"You're obviously afraid of him?" His face darkened.

"Jude, I'm waiting for him to turn up one day," she confessed.

He reached out and took her hand. "If you're afraid of him why don't you do something about it?"

"Like what? Take out a restraining order? They don't work. Much better to hide."

"Is that why you're here?" He shook her fingers as though he wanted to shake it out of her. "You're hiding out?"

"Tony and I worked it out between us. He knew what had happened to my mother. He was devastated but I never told him what was happening to me. I didn't even understand what was happening—I told you I was a real mess. It seemed it was impossible to get through to anyone outside Deborah. Everyone admired him you see, he was—is—Professor Lundberg, and he gave lots of money to the university."

He could well see how it was. "So where were you before you came here? The years in-between?"

"I've been a gypsy," She laughed. Not a happy sound. "I've never been in any one place for any length of time except for two years as a governess on an Outback station. I was safe there. I'm safe here. Or so I thought before Ralph Rogan arrived, and then you turned up with your mind-blowing news."

"Which we haven't really touched on."

"Not tonight." It sounded like a plea. "I just can't handle it tonight."

"Okay. And this business with the crystals?"

"My Outback friends and my own wanderings. Eventually I started to make good overseas contacts. People have been so kind and helpful to me. People who love crystals generally love people. Perhaps the crystals influence their lives. I've learned such a lot."

"Why did you leave?" he asked, wanting to find out every last thing about her.

She shrugged evasively. "The children, a boy and a girl, twins, went away to boarding school. I had to move on or stay and marry someone. There's a shortage of women in the bush, but marriage isn't on my agenda."

"Why not?"

There was a profound sadness in her face. "I'm a bit like you, Jude. I don't think I could ever trust anyone enough to marry them."

"There's a statement, Cate."

"I can't change how I feel. Trust is something that has been stolen from me. But somehow you've reached me. Maybe it's because you know all about heartbreak." She lifted her face to the sparkling stars. "I think I'll go to bed, if that's okay with you? I feel really odd, all keyed up yet exhausted. I don't seem to be able to take in all that's happening. In fact I have no idea what the heck is going on."

"Me, either," he declared.

The light caught in his blond hair. In the balmy salt air it was a mass of tousled waves and curls. She had actually felt those waves and curls beneath her hands. It was a source of wonder. She thought she might be coming seriously adrift.

"Tomorrow when you're feeling better we'll have to discuss the will."

"I don't want his money, Jude," Cate said, beginning to gather up the coffee cups and saucers. "I don't even want to discuss it. To tell you the truth, I don't actually believe it. Lester Rogan was nothing to me, I swear. The only reason he came into my life was as my landlord.''

''For all that he's left you what most people including me would consider a fortune.''

She didn't even ask how much. It didn't belong to her anyway. ''I'll take getting my mother back, Jude,'' she said sadly and turned away.

There were rough times ahead.

CHAPTER FIVE

THE HOUSE was silent when he woke up. He turned his head to check on the bedside clock. The digital display told him it was almost half eight. God, he'd slept in. Why wouldn't he? With Cate half way down the corridor he hadn't drifted off like a baby. He'd tossed and turned for hours, his body in a high state of arousal. Not remarkable after those passionate kisses. She shouldn't have laughed like that, she shouldn't have parted her mouth for him.

"Come on, Jude buddy, get up!" He issued himself the instruction.

There was movement in the grounds, the murmur of voices. He pulled on a pair of shorts, ran a hand over his unruly hair and walked to the balcony.

"Jimmy, that you down there?"

A moment later Jimmy appeared from beneath the balcony, a nuggety little man with a shiny brown nut of a pate. "Howya goin' there, me boy?" He gave Jude a huge conspiratorial wink.

"You're early!"

"You've been in the city too long, son. I've been up since five. I've got Catey with me."

"Have you now?"

Cate appeared, dressed in the same sarong-type skirt with a different top, sleeveless, low-neck, yellow to match the yellow hibiscus on her multicoloured skirt.

"Good morning!" She turned a smiling face up to him. "Jimmy's been keeping me company."

93

"Enjoying meself," said Jimmy with relish. "Ya betta come down, son. Catey's starvin', aren't ya love?"

"I am now. The admiral Jimmy has brought fresh croissants and little Danish pastries from the bake shop," she told Jude, reaching out to pick an avocado off a tree, cradling it in her hand. "I love avocados."

"Then you'll have to try me guacamole, Catey, with home made tortilla," Jimmy suggested helpfully. "I use pita bread at a pinch. I reckon no one makes it better," he added modestly. "I've had it tons of times in the West Indies when I go over for the cricket. 'Struth, seems to me those West Indians eat avocados at ever meal. Bigger ones than that, love. They breed 'em huge! You oughta try me guacamole with poached chicken and a cumin flavoured sauce."

"Only if you cook it, Jimmy," she teased.

"You're on. Are ya comin' down, son?" Jimmy peered up at Jude again.

"Sure. Give me five minutes."

He made it in less, face splashed with cold water, hair brushed, a white T-shirt to team with his shorts.

Jimmy was reclining in a sea grass chair in the family room adjoining the kitchen, while Cate was busy making the coffee. "Catey has been tellin' me about last night," Jimmy said with an expression of great disgust.

Jude shot her a quick glance. "Okay, Cate, what did you tell?"

"Nuthin' about you two, you galah," Jimmy reassured him with rough affection. "That brute of a Ralph! A real bastard like his dad. Now there was a guy who hated his fellow man."

Cate set the coffee to perk. "I've got a big surprise for you, Jimmy," she offered wryly. "Lester Rogan left me a lot of money which gave Ralph a very good reason to come calling."

Jimmy sat up, looking dumbfounded. He tore his eyes away from Cate to stare at Jude. "What is that all about? Ya not going to tell me Les finally turned religious?"

"Come on, Jimmy, we both know Lester wasn't a practising Christian," Jude scoffed. "The fact is Cate claims to have no idea why Lester left her the bulk of his fortune."

The astounding news set up a facial tick beneath Jimmy's right eye. He leapt to his feet curling his fingers strongly around Jude's arm. "Jude, me old mate, the worst word in that sentence is "claims." If Catey says she doesn't know why Les left her the whole caboodle she doesn't."

It was Jimmy in champion mode. All he needed was a crusader's cape, Jude thought. "Legal word, Jimmy," he said, only half humorously. Jimmy's wry fingers had the grip of a sand crab.

"Isn't that just typical Les!" Jimmy exclaimed, letting go of Jude's arm. "I swear he hated Ralph more'an Ralph hated him. You're not gunna tell me Les left poor old Myra out in the cold? A lost soul if ever there was one. What a life of wedded bliss she's had with Les! What about Melly? I ask ya, is she ever gunna grow up? And Ralph, always snarling. He is the man's only son however. Les surely didn't forget about them?"

Jude's gaze moved in Cate's direction. She was giving all her attention to setting the table. Or so it seemed. In the centre was a copper bowl filled with vibrant orange hibiscus. He loved little touches like that even if they did remind him of his mother. She had one tucked into her hair. "They've all been extremely well provided for if you don't count the fact they're the man's family. It never occurred to any of them, including me they wouldn't get the lot."

"Ya dad knew," Jimmy scratched his bald pate. "I wonder what he made of it."

''You bet your life he didn't think Lester had gone senile.''

''And Matty told no one?''

''It would have been unethical for him to do so, Jimmy. You know that.''

''This is amazing. I'm gobsmacked.''

''We all are, Jimmy,'' Cate said dryly. ''In fact I feel threatened. That's why I'm here with Jude.''

''A real gentleman is Jude,'' Jimmy smiled a big smile. ''I hope he stays that way,'' he cackled.

Jude laughed. Jimmy looked as though he knew what Jude's night had been like.

''European style breakfast this morning,'' Cate informed them. ''Come along now. It's ready.''

''Have you made me tea, love?'' Jimmy asked. ''Coffee brings on cardiac arrest.''

''I already knew to make tea for you, Jimmy.'' Cate reassured him, bringing the teapot to the table. ''Coffee for the two of us, Jude. Okay?''

''Fine.'' He held her chair while she slid into it.

''Gee, these look good. Melt in the mouth,'' Jimmy said, helping himself to a croissant. ''I suppose they're life-threatening as well. Everything you read tells you to stop eatin' this, stop eatin' that. Which, I'm pleased to say I mostly ignore. So…'' He buttered his buttery croissant lavishly, then added a big scoop of his own cumquat marmalade. ''Nuthin' occurs to you, love, about Les?''

Cate shook her head. ''No. I have no idea why he named me in his will. I look on it more as a disaster than a miracle, Jimmy. You've come into the gallery—''

''Barged in more like it,'' Jimmy interjected.

''When Mr Rogan was there,'' Cate finished off.

''Wasn't gunna leave you alone with that old lecher,'' Jimmy explained, his voice dripping disgust.

NO POSTAGE
NECESSARY
IF MAILED
IN THE
UNITED STATES

BUSINESS REPLY MAIL

FIRST-CLASS MAIL   PERMIT NO. 717-003   BUFFALO, NY

POSTAGE WILL BE PAID BY ADDRESSEE

HARLEQUIN READER SERVICE
3010 WALDEN AVE
PO BOX 1867
BUFFALO NY 14240-9952

Get FREE BOOKS and a FREE GIFT when you play the...

LAS VEGAS GAME

Just scratch off the gold box with a coin. Then check below to see the gifts you get!

YES! I have scratched off the gold Box. Please send me my **2 FREE BOOKS** and **gift for which I qualify.** I understand that I am under no obligation to purchase any books as explained on the back of this card.

▲ DETACH AND MAIL CARD TODAY! ▲

386 HDL DZ9U   186 HDL D2AA

FIRST NAME	LAST NAME

ADDRESS

APT.#	CITY

STATE/PROV.	ZIP/POSTAL CODE

(H-R-07/04)

7	7	7	Worth TWO FREE BOOKS plus a BONUS Mystery Gift!
🍒	🍒	🍒	Worth TWO FREE BOOKS!
🔔	🔔	♣	TRY AGAIN!

www.eHarlequin.com

Cate looked straight into Jude's narrowed, watchful eyes. "I promise you I never saw that side of Lester Rogan. I never saw him as an ageing Casanova."

Jimmy scoffed. "Les could have given Casanova lessons."

"Please, Jimmy, you've never really listened to me," Cate pleaded. "It wasn't like that at all."

"No, it wasn't me, darlin'." Jimmy fired up. "Lester was smart enough to register I was right on to him. Me and Gwennie."

Jude's eyebrows shot up. "You can't mean Miss Forsyth?"

"The very same person," Jimmy said with satisfaction. "Gwennie and me have been keepin' our eye on Cate since she arrived in town."

"You've no idea how kind they've been," Cate looked toward Jude, the sweetest expression on her face. He wouldn't have been human if that smile didn't make some of his anxieties melt.

"Watchin' over her like a couple of guardian angels," Jimmy said, looking happy. "Oh my, won't Gwennie be shocked! We thought we were protectin' Cate from Les now he's gone and left her a bloody fortune. Gwennie will want to start up an investigation. Ya know what's she's like."

Jude was forced to smother another laugh. Gwennie was Miss Gwendoline Forsyth—town character who claimed to have regular out of body experiences—former teacher of English, History (Modern and Ancient) Speech and Drama, at Saint Agatha's private school for girls in Cairns, until her retirement. That had to be over a decade ago, putting "Gwennie" square in her seventies. "I think the two of you better leave that to me," Jude suggested. "How is Miss Forsyth these days? Still doing her astral travelling?"

Jimmy laughed. "With clouds for her magic carpets. She

was in Tibet the other day, she and the Dalai Lama were burning incense together. She's fine. She still goes runnin' on the beach and she's seventy-five.''

"She's a running-walking advertisement for exercise,'' Cate laughed. "I just hope I look and feel as good if I ever get to Miss Forsyth's age.''

"And she's got perfect teeth,'' Jimmy said, sounding proud. "Look at me I've got fillings.'' He opened his mouth and tapped his back teeth. "None of which helps Cate here. What are we gunna do about Ralph?'' Jimmy addressed Jude while Cate refilled Jimmy's empty cup. "We can't have him botherin' Cate.''

"No, we can't,'' Jude clipped off. "Cate needs protecting. I'll sort it out, Jimmy. It'd be a huge help if we could establish the connection between Lester and Cate. There has to be one. So, Cate—'' he looked across the table at her "—I need to go over a few things with you, including letting you read the will. You were too upset last night.''

"I'll go if you want to talk privately,'' Jimmy offered helpfully, regarding one then the other.

Cate shook her head. "No, Jimmy. Please stay. Jude may be stopping just short of saying it, but I know he's sceptical.''

"He is a lawyer, darlin','' Jimmy snorted.

"I've got nothing to tell.'' Cate spread her hands.

"Why did you come up here, Catey?'' Jimmy asked earnestly. "Ya never did tell us. Gwennie reckons you must be on the run from somebody. A beautiful girl like you burying herself in a little sugar town.''

"This is magnificent country, Jimmy,'' Cate protested, meeting his eyes. "Where the rain forest meets the reef, isn't that it? I enjoy the peace and the beauty, I love my gallery. I sell quite a bit when the tourists come into town.''

"Ah, darlin', you could be a movie star,'' Jimmy chortled, an admiring look on his face, tanned to the texture of soft leather. "I'm an old man seventy and more and I can't take me eyes off ya. She's beautiful, isn't she?" Jimmy appealed to the silent Jude.

"And mysterious." Jude shot Cate a sapphire glance.

"Look, I think I should go." Jimmy rose to his feet. "That tea was lovely, Catey. You make it just right. It's an art, you know. You two need to talk. What about if I ask Gwennie to join us at lunch, Jude? Cate must come of course."

"That's nice of you, Jimmy, but I really should open the gallery," Cate responded, sounding not all that determined.

"Struth, love, you're rich!" Jimmy burst out laughing. "You can afford to come to lunch. Gwennie knows more about the Rogans than anyone. She taught poor little Mel and I know Myra used to confide in her. Gwennie has to be the best listener in the world. She might be able to see some connection?"

Jude's expression was doubtful. "When did Lester Rogan settle in the district exactly? He was around all my life, Ralph and I are the same age."

Jimmy scratched his polished pate. "It had to be a year or two before he married Myra. We were all placing bets on which local girl he was gunna choose. Not that Myra wasn't pretty in those days but it helped a lot her dad was makin' quite a bit of money buyin' and sellin' land. He was one of our first developers as a matter of fact. He was the one who got Les into the business, though Les didn't come up here penniless like most young fellas. He had money behind him even then. From where I don't know. Never talked about a family. Not as far as I know. Gwennie might remember something. She was invited to the weddin'. I wasn't. I wasn't far enough up the social scale. Ya mum and dad went."

Jude's expression momentarily darkened, imagining his father thinking he was going to be happily married forever. "Ask Miss Forsyth by all means," he said eventually. "I'd love to see her again. She might be able to clear up a few things as well. Okay with you, Cate?"

"We need all the help we can get, don't we?" Cate answered, nodding her head.

Let's hope it's something you can live with, Jude prayed.

On his way to the front door Jimmy turned back to Jude with a question. "A table for four at Elio's? Inside, or out?"

"Out," Jude nodded. "I like it in the courtyard. Make it for 1:00 p.m."

"Ya won't know me, Catey, when you see me wearin' some nice duds!" Jimmy promised.

"I'll look forward to it," Cate was still smiling when she began stacking the cups, saucers and plates. "We ate every last crumb of Jimmy's welcome offering," she said lightly, aware of the seriousness of Jude's expression. "I'll need to go back home." She moved towards the kitchen. "I can't hide out here forever."

"I suppose not." Not if he had to continue to hold her at arm's length. Cate Costello was the most powerfully intriguing woman he had ever met. "This whole business is very odd." He turned his head so he could continue to look at her. "People don't leave a fortune to total strangers, or near enough."

"They just leave it to dog's homes, cat's homes and the like," she offered half flippantly.

"People who do that generally have no one else in the world. Lester Rogan had a family."

"Yet he bequeathed the bulk of his fortune to me." She swept her hair back over her shoulder, a sure sign of agitation. "Do you think I can see the will please?"

"Of course. I'll go get it." Jude heard the edginess in her

voice. He was feeling more than a little on edge himself. For someone who had laboured to maintain a fail-safe self assured facade Cate with very little effort was putting him into a spin.

When he returned with the document he placed it in her hand. "Go to Page Two."

"Thank you." She wandered back into the living room, taking a chair at the glass-topped table. Every now and again she looked up at him, her expression grave. "This will was made over two years ago. Before I even came here. It revokes all other wills."

"Yes," Jude confirmed briefly. Ralph had previously been the main beneficiary.

"It says here I own land, houses, buildings. Even the gallery is mine—"

"Money, everything."

She shook her head helplessly. "He gave no indication he would ever do such a thing."

"Tell me again what you talked about?"

He sounded calm and courteous but Cate wasn't happy with the glitter in his eyes. "Jude, what good would that do?"

"Let me decide. He asked you about your childhood; your mother, your father, your stepfather, your entire life before you fled up here?"

She stared into his handsome, charming face, seeing another side to him. The professional. "Why do you give me the strong impression you're not believing a word I say?"

"That's not true!" He angled his dark golden head at her. "But I need answers, Cate. You need to come up with them."

She shook her head almost angrily. "I've told you I don't have any answers."

Jude took a seat opposite her, holding up a palm. "You're

not telling me everything, Cate. I'm sure there are some things you prefer left in the dark.''

''Like what?'' she asked, a warning brightness in her eyes. ''Next you're going to say I was sleeping with Lester Rogan.''

''Were you?'' he asked bluntly.

She made to jump up, but he reached out and held her fine narrow wrist, not applying any pressure, but locking it all the same. ''Cate?'' he asked quietly.

''You're working on that assumption and I bitterly resent it,'' she said, waiting for him to remove his hand. Such a disturbing sensation. Warm, tingling, never bruising. ''Lester Rogan may have been a lustful man but he didn't act that way around me.''

''So there was nothing sexual?''

''How many times do I have to tell you,'' she asked in despair.

''Forgive me, but I have to come up with something to put the brakes on the Rogan family. You saw Ralph in action. He's in a very dangerous mood.''

She looked away. ''He chilled my blood, and on the subject of 'sexual' if you hadn't arrived I doubt if he would have backed off. He's a pig.''

''Sure. You don't have to convince me. Running through our options, next on the agenda is a blood tie. You don't see that as a possibility?''

Her green eyes filled with something like horror. ''Until I came up here I'd never seen Lester Rogan before in my life.''

''Tell me about your parents,'' he invited quietly. ''Start with your mother. I know it's a terribly painful subject but can you try? Would your mother have known Lester Rogan at some stage of her life?''

''No, she wouldn't,'' Cate moaned in frustration.

"How would you know? For all his faults and failings Lester Rogan as a young man would have been a pretty impressive looking guy. Plenty of girls hang around Ralph for that matter."

"That's a mystery to me," Cate said acidly. "I think he's horrible. I can't think my mother would ever have been involved with someone like Lester Rogan. She was only twenty when she married my father. Tony on his own admission loved her and wanted to marry her but she gave her heart to Dad."

"What was your mother's maiden name?" Jude asked

Cate rose from the table quickly. "I'm sorry, Jude, but I can't talk about my mother. It's all too raw and alive."

"Please."

"Courtney."

He stared up at her. "Please try to bear with me for just a moment. She was born in Australia?"

"Yes. My father wasn't. I told you last night, he was born in Ireland. He was a clever, cultured man, a gentleman. I was so proud of him."

"I wonder if it's possible he knew Lester Rogan?" Jude mused.

"They weren't in prison together if that's what you mean?" Cate countered sharply, visibly becoming more upset by the moment. "You're a lawyer, Jude, not a policeman."

"I'm sorry. I don't want to upset you but lawyers and policeman have something in common. They both have to carry out investigations. We're trying to establish the link between you or some member of your family to Lester Rogan. Surely Rogan's an Irish name? Rogan, Regan, Reagan?"

"So what?" She sat down again, staring at him. "Irish immigrants poured into Australia. There are more Irish outside Ireland than in. Nearly everyone here, apart from Asian migrants, have antecedents from England, Ireland or Scotland. Lester Rogan had a broad Australian accent. He may have been very rich but he didn't speak like an educated man. I suppose you would have to call him a rough diamond. My father had a lovely speaking voice. I can't see any connection whatever to Rogan. I'd like to go home, Jude.''

The room seemed very still. Just the two of them trying to absorb what was happening to them, neither able to put aside that inflammatory incident on the beach. "I'll take you.''

"I'm sorry if I sound ungrateful.''

Abruptly Jude pushed his chair back and stood up. Just looking at her he experienced an upsurge of primitive desire that shocked him. He had to move to curb it. Losing control could turn out to be disastrous. This beautiful creature had suffered enough. "We do have to talk, Cate.'' He reverted to his professional voice. "I have to say as well, I'm not at all happy about your staying at the gallery at night.''

"I don't have any option.'' She willed her voice not to tremble. Ralph Rogan had frightened her and she didn't frighten easily. Her mind seized on an image of him lumbering towards her, the scraping sound of his shoes, that peculiar look in his eyes.

"I repeat, you can stay here.'' Maybe he was too chivalrous for his own good? What did he really know about Cate Costello beyond the fact she was so beautiful and so poignant she made his heart melt. Then there was her traumatic background, the mystery of her mother's disappearance, the questions hanging over the stepfather. Had the stepfather been instrumental in the mother's disappearance or were Cate's suspicions fuelled by distrust and dislike?

There were dangerous and disturbing depths to the whole story.

"You'll be quite safe," he tacked on when she didn't speak.

"Will I?" She gave a brittle little laugh. "You're not looking for an affair, are you, Jude? Something to tide you over the holidays?"

"That would mess things up good and proper wouldn't it?" he said harshly. "I'm attracted to you, Cate. I can't hide that. Not after last night, but I have a job to do. I don't want you back at the gallery for a very good reason. Even if he was warned off by me and the police, I don't think Ralph would have the brains to stay away. To make it worse, he drinks. He's been getting drunk since he was fourteen years old."

"So you think he'd harm me?"

"Cate, you think so, too."

"Maybe I could stay with Miss Forsyth?" She bit her lip, considering." I know she'd take me in at the drop of a hat. She and Jimmy have been very kind and supportive."

"So you're scared of me?" he asked with a half smile.

She looked into his sizzling blue eyes trying to fathom her exact emotions towards him. "What do you expect me to say, I'd rather be with you?"

"Well…I come with the house. There's plenty of room here. As I recall Miss Forsyth's place is pretty much on the small side. I'm sure she's filled it with her amazing cats. She's a teeny weeny bit crazy, you know."

Cate's tense expression eased into a smile. "Eccentric," she corrected. "Aren't you worried Rogan might come here? Knowing you were sheltering me would make him very angry."

"Angrier than he is already?" Jude raised a mocking brow. "Don't worry, I'm sure the last time Ralph and I came to blows is still fresh in his memory. We don't have to discuss it right now. Let's get you home."

CHAPTER SIX

FIFTEEN minutes later Jude turned off the beach road and into the cul-de-sac where Cate had her gallery. She no longer had to rent it, he thought. It was hers thanks to Lester Rogan. To any reasonable mind that bespoke a connection Cate up to date had vehemently denied. There was nothing unusual about that, he'd often had to wade through client's lies and omissions, but to this day Cate Costello was the most mysterious of them all. She no longer needed to work...it had fallen to him to confirm overnight she had become a multimillionairess. That should solve all her financial problems for a lifetime. But she had other huge problems. Top of the list, the previously cited main beneficiary, Ralph Rogan, Lester's only son.

The instant they pulled into the parking bay Cate turned to him. She was all eyes and delicate high cheekbones, her soft luscious mouth free of lipstick. For some reason he found that incredibly erotic. The now familiar throb of desire started up in his loins. Was it possible a woman could reach out and touch not only a man's body but his heart and soul? The worst possible scenario was she could be playing him like a flute.

"I don't want to go in." The expression on her face held more than a trace of alarm.

He smiled, endeavouring to humour her. "I can understand that, Cate, but we have to. You want to check on things...change for lunch."

"He's been here." A little frisson rippled visibly through her body.

"You mean again?" He caught her mood, tried to steady her with a hand on her shoulder. "If you don't want to go in, stay here. Let me check it out."

"No, we'll go together." She hesitated only a moment. She unbuckled her seat belt and sprang out of the car with near kinetic energy making not towards the gallery entrance but the rear of the house.

Jude sprinted after her thinking it was becoming a habit. He closed in on her, making sure he was first to pound onto the deck.

"Is everything okay?" She waited at the bottom of the steps, staring up at him, a little breathless, holding her side. Her whole body was tense as piano wire.

He looked through the picture windows, cold anger sweeping over him. Even knowing Ralph and what he was capable of he could scarcely believe his eyes. "Stay here," he said sharply.

The back door had been jemmied open. It gave with the slightest push. Inside was pandemonium. The place had been ransacked. There was not a piece of furniture that hadn't been disturbed or thrown over. The large book case at the far end of the room was built in otherwise Jude was sure it would have been sent crashing to the polished floor. As it was, the books were scattered, some obviously flung, all over the room. It was immediately clear Ralph had taken his revenge.

By the time Jude walked into the bedroom, involuntarily sucking in his breath in anticipation of what he might find, Cate was at his side. She stared in horror at the upheaval. Her clothes had been dragged out of the walk-in wardrobes and flung to the floor. Drawers had been pulled out of chests the contents spilled. Ornaments were smashed. Inexplicably the portrait of her as a girl had escaped any sort of violation.

No accounting for that, Jude thought, when so much other damage had been done.

The bathroom was heavy with scents from the contents of a variety of broken bottles that littered the tiles; perfume, bath salts, mouthwash, fragments of blue and white porcelain from bathroom accessories. One quick look then Cate turned around with a strangled cry making for the gallery. There was a very strong lock on the door. She had the key.

As she opened it Jude felt the knot in his stomach tighten. There were only two ways into the gallery. Through the front door which she'd had the sense to fit with a wrought-iron security door, and this rear door opening into the living quarters. With any luck at all Ralph or his hireling—that had to be considered—hadn't been able to get so far.

Cate snapped on the lights, transforming the gallery into a fireworks of coloured light. "Thank God!" she moaned, in relief.

Jude stared around him, initially with answering relief then fascination that temporarily overrode his shocked anger. He remembered the gallery from Tony Mandel's day, but Cate had transformed the white walled art gallery into a glittering crystal cave. The interior had become a kaleidoscope of colours as the recessed lighting fell upon myriad shapes and designs; chunks of aquamarine, amethyst, rose quartz, obsidian, the extraordinary glitter of fool's gold, other shades of purple, orange, yellow, green, deep violet shot with a lovely blue colour. The crystals were ranged all around the room, adorning the long shelves fixed to the walls, and artistically positioned on free-standing pyramids and circular towers made out of chrome with white marble shelving. It was another world. A world filled with treasures from the earth.

"This is extraordinary," he said. "Beautiful!"

"Thank you." She was drawn to stare into his handsome

face as though it were a magnet; as though there was no one else in the world to cling to. She could still taste his mouth, this near stranger. See his face when she closed her eyes.

"We have to be grateful he couldn't get in," Jude's blue eyes were still glued to the crystal collection. "Or maybe he was disturbed. It's Ralph's work of course, Ralph or someone he hired to do his dirty work for him. It wouldn't be the first time. Then again Ralph might have derived maximum satisfaction from doing the job himself. We'll have to call in the police, Cate. He can't be allowed to get away with this."

Her stunned anger was quickly passing into a desperate need for caution. "Or we could simply ignore it. Keep quiet," she suggested.

Jude shook his head emphatically. "I'd feel a whole lot better if we let the police take a look at this."

"What if it wasn't Ralph?" A shadow fell across her face.

He made a little jeering sound. "Who else, Cate? After what's happened."

"He wants us to call the police. He wants the whole story to come out. He wants the town to feel sorry for him and angry with me. He won't be caught anyway, he'll have a water-tight alibi for where he was last night. Off the top of my head he'd say he spent the night with some girl. She'll swear to it."

He flashed her a sardonic glance. "I know all about Ralph and his friends. I've known for years. His DNA would be all over the house. Of course he could account for that from his previous visit." He added with regret.

"Exactly. I don't want to call in the police, Jude. I want to keep this quiet."

She seemed genuinely panicked. He wanted to draw her

into his arms, wipe that urgent look of appeal off her face. "You've got an enemy, Cate. There's a big flaw in your decision. Next time he'll target the gallery. Think of all the damage he could do, that's some collection!"

She, too, looked around the gallery; at the beautiful crystals she had arranged so artistically. "I'm glad you like it. Surely I can have a security system fitted today? Or as soon as possible. I should have done it at the beginning when I first came here."

"That would have been a good idea."

"Everyone seemed so friendly, so open and honest. He couldn't afford to smash the front windows. The Harveys aren't that far away, they would have heard it. Surely he didn't come back in that flashy red sports car?"

Jude shrugged. "It's the closest he's got to a getaway car. Maybe he wore some kind of disguise," he suggested acidly. "A baseball cap pulled down over his eyes, sunglasses, a goatee beard. Ralph's none too bright. Then again he could have had one of his social misfit friends do the job for him. Sounds reasonable given your portrait wasn't touched. Maybe the guy who broke in didn't recognise you as the subject? It's very beautiful, by the way."

Cate nodded. "Tony is a gifted artist. I would have been terribly upset if the painting had been damaged. It has great sentimental value for me."

"And monetary value," he pointed out dryly.

"It's Tony's work," she said, turning away from his keen eyes knowing he was struggling to make sense of her and her story. "I'll feel better once I clear up."

Jude glanced at his watch. "I'd better cancel lunch."

"You go." She turned her face back to him.

"Don't be ridiculous." He didn't intend it but his voice was close to brusque. "I still think you should call the police, Cate. You must establish there's been a break-in."

She tucked a long swing of copper hair behind her ear. "Please, Jude, I don't want to." She was so acutely aware of him it made her nerves jump.

"Why do I have this constant feeling you're holding something back?" he demanded.

She shut her eyes tight, small white teeth gritted. "I'm not. Believe me. I better get started."

He reached into his pocket for his cell phone. "Give me a minute to ring Jimmy, then I'll help you. Keep out of the bathroom with all that broken glass. I'll take care of that job."

"What kind of a bastard would do this?" Jimmy asked, looking around him at the senseless mess.

"I'll give you a clue, Jimmy," Jude said, his expression grim. "It starts with an R. You're looking at the result of a half an hour's clean-up work by the two of us. You should have seen it when we came in. We've just finished putting the books back."

"And he's gone and broken ya lovely lamp, Catey!" Jimmy mourned. "I can't understand why you don't want to talk to the police, love. Bennett's a good bloke. They're there to protect you."

"Jude has done a good job so far." She smiled in Jude's direction but he didn't smile back.

He held up his hands. "I wanted her to report it as well."

"Now the gallery would have been the real prize," Jimmy mused.

Jude shrugged. "Too much of a risk putting a brick through the front window. Thankfully Cate went to the trouble of putting an excellent lock on the door leading into the gallery. Or I guess Ralph could have thought enough is enough, leave the gallery for next time. This could be the start of a campaign."

"Yeah, well…" Jimmy scratched his bald head. "We can throw a spoke in that."

"You bet we can!" Jude rasped. "I've called in Hazletts to fix up a few surprises including a surveillance camera." Jude righted a couple of bar stools. "Cate can afford it now," he added dryly. "He should be here shortly."

"So what can I do?" Jimmy asked. "He's a miserable son of a bitch, that Ralph. A coward, too. He's got a couple of no-hopers among his mates. Could have been that guy, Kramer. Drop-out. Leads a useless existence. Could have done it for a price. Kramer doesn't fit in with most folks but Ralph keeps him in his entourage."

"I'll be sure to ask Ralph when I see him later in the day," Jude said in a voice full of intent. "You can help me here, Jimmy, if you like, while Cate gets busy in the bedroom."

"Fine." Jimmy lost no time getting to work.

Miss Forsyth was uncharacteristically speechless when she surveyed the chaos in the bedroom.

"I respect the fact you want to keep this quiet, m'dear, but I have to tell you I side with Jude and Jimmy on this. I think you should have called in the police. Someone has to teach Ralph Rogan a lesson."

Cate looked back at the tall, spare, elderly lady who had befriended her. Miss Forsyth was impeccably dressed in what Cate thought of as her "daytime uniform." Today it was one of her pristine long-sleeved pin-tucked white cotton shirts with a Nehru collar worn loose over baggy beige linen slacks, tan leather sandals on her feet. Her woolly snow-white hair that had in her youth been a riot of tight chestnut curls was drawn up and back into a knot. Her facial bones were very prominent, balancing the distinguished beak of a nose. Cate felt a surge of affection for her. "He has been taught a lesson, Miss Forsyth,'' she said. "By his father. I know Jimmy can't hold anything back from you, so you'll be aware I'm Lester Rogan's main beneficiary.''

Miss Forsyth gave a genteel sniff. "It's the kind of surprise that could cause one to drop dead of a heart attack.'' She reached down to pick up a few dresses still on their hangers. "There's something I need to ask you, m'dear. Did you already know Lester and were forced to keep quiet?''

Cate returned Miss Forsyth's shrewd gaze. "I never heard of Lester Rogan before I came to this town. I've been over and over this with Jude. He's been very kind even when I feel he hardly believes a word I say.''

"A true gentleman is Jude,'' Miss Forsyth nodded approvingly. "As for not believing you, you must consider it is an odd story. But odd stories are the best of all. There has to be a connection, you're just missing it.''

"Try as I might I can't think of it, Miss Forsyth,'' Cate assured her, walking back and forth from the bed to the wardrobe.

Miss Forsyth crouched down to pick up some scattered T-shirts. "In one of these drawers, dear?''

"The top one, Miss Forsyth. You don't have to do anything. Please, sit down.''

"I'm not in my element doing nothing.'' Miss Forsyth began folding the tops neatly and placing them in the top drawer of the teak chest. "Let's face it. The will has made Ralph very, very angry. That is to be expected. It's not something any family would want to hear. He was such a cruel man, Lester. He gave his family such a bad time. That's when they saw him. He was away from home such a lot, supposedly working on his deals but I suspect he was getting up to a whole lot of things more exotic.''

Cate paused in what she was doing to look back at Miss Forsyth with perplexity. "Like what?''

Miss Forsyth shrugged a shoulder. "Lester started up re-lationships at the drop of a hat. Myra had a very difficult job trying to track him down. In time she learned not to bother. I shouldn't be surprised if Lester Rogan had off-spring all over the place."

"Well don't look at me," Cate said, feeling like she was actually in limbo. "My mother loved my father. He was the only man in her life."

"I'm sure, m'dear. Don't get upset. We're talking hy-pothcticals."

"Besides, I already told Jude I resemble my father's side of the family. I have his colouring. That's settles it as far as I'm concerned, if it even needed settling. The connection doesn't lie there. Why he was so nice to me, I don't know. Why he left me the bulk of his fortune I don't know, either. I'm not happy about it. I don't want his money. I know you and Jimmy were worried every time he came into the gallery but he just wanted to talk."

Miss Forsyth spoke in a calm, soothing voice. "What were you talking about? Go ahead, my dear. Tell me," she urged. "I'm listening. I only want to help you."

Cate shrugged helplessly. "I know that. But it's as I've told you before, Miss Forsyth. It was mostly general con-versation. We spoke about the crystals, their properties. He was very interested in them and he bought a number of pieces. He liked to hear about my time in the Outback as a governess."

"Did he manage to coax out of you your history?" Miss Forsyth asked, staring at Cate thoughtfully.

Cate flushed. "I told him a little about my childhood. My mother and father. Not much. We spoke about Tony, of course. Tony sold him the gallery, which it appears is now mine."

Miss Forsyth lay down a garment she was folding and

refolding without much thought. She looked at Cate across the bed. "Why is it you don't speak about your past life, m'dear? We respect your privacy of course, but you know you're among friends. Surely you can trust us? There must be a connection somewhere for Lester to have written you into his will. One could almost conclude you are family in some way. That could be a vital key to the mystery."

"No way, Miss Forsyth." Cate took a deep steadying breath. "Honestly. No way either was I Lester Rogan's toy girl."

Miss Forsyth gave a disgusted click of her tongue. "That's not a point we need cleared up, m'dear. I would never have thought that in a million years."

"I think it's crossed Jude's mind," Cate said unhappily.

"That upsets you obviously." Miss Forsyth flashed another of her razor-sharp grey glances.

"Definitely."

"I must tuck that to the back of my mind. Jude's a lawyer, m'dear, executor of the estate, he's obliged to think of everything. I'm sure it only took him another ten seconds to realise that theory is out of the question. I have a feeling it could have something to do with your parents. Whatever his failings Lester was perfectly rational, not demented. This puzzle has a logic to it, a verifiable explanation. Who is it who can help you?"

Cate sat down on the side of the bed, hugging her slender body with her arms. "My parents can't tell me anything, Miss Forsyth. I'm an orphan just as I told you."

Miss Forsyth shook her head, clearly seeing herself in the role of detective. "You're an orphan now, Cate—I am so sorry such a thing had to happen to you—but you and your parents had a life together. Somehow Lester Rogan was tucked away in the past. He might have known your parents before you were old enough to remember him. The connec-

tion must have been very strong to survive all these years.
Lester was not a doer of good deeds. He was no philan-
thropist, he was a mean man, he enjoyed being mean. He
enjoyed cracking the whip over his family. Maybe this inheritance is in the nature of retribution. Lester knew for a
couple of years he was a prime candidate for a heart attack
or stroke. Finally he may have wanted to put his life in
order.''

Cate sighed. ''What a pity he couldn't have taken into
account all the upset his will would cause. He would have
known his family's reaction, how shocked they would be,
outraged might be a better word. And what about me?
Didn't he consider he might be exposing me to actual dan-
ger? He knew his own son. I've heard Ralph Rogan has a
job controlling his temper at the best of times.''

Miss Forsyth too sat down, collapsing lightly into an armchair, a flush perhaps of intuition crossing her papery
cheeks. ''Maybe Lester badly wanted to make amends without letting any skeletons out of the closet, m'dear?''

Cate couldn't answer for a moment. She felt like a few
skeletons were watching her right now. ''What he has
done,'' she said finally, ''is put me at risk.''

The security man took some time installing the new system.
The rest of them, Jude and Cate, Miss Forsyth and Jimmy
worked together to restore order, Miss Forsyth powering
along like a woman in her thirties. She even made the suggestion with the air of confident assertion that was so much
a part of her that she would make sandwiches for lunch.

No one refused and in no time at all, a very interesting
selection appeared, arranged in a gingham lined basket. She
had consulted no one regarding the fillings choosing them
all herself from what Cate had in the frig and the pantry.
Both areas mercifully hadn't figured in the attack which

turned out to be a real bonus. There were chicken and avocado triple deckers with a pat of mayonnaise and a sprinkle of chopped walnuts, crab meat and cream cheese, paper thin turkey breast with ginger and mango chutney and a few sprigs of rocket, all washed down with very good iced tea. They were all hungry. Afterwards Jimmy draped an arm around Miss Forsyth, bending to peck her noisily on the cheek.

"I wouldn't be a bit surprised if one of these days we end up married, Gwennie?"

She laughed. "Wishful thinking, Jimmy. I'm too set in my ways not that you're at all serious. You know I'm never likely to say yes—much better to be friends."

"Spoken by a woman who climbed out of a bathroom window on her wedding day," Jimmy chortled.

Cate couldn't tell if Jimmy was joking or not. "Did you really, Miss Forsyth?"

"No. Absolutely not." Miss Forsyth prodded Jimmy hard in the chest. "How dare you try to soil my reputation, Jimmy. I climbed out the bathroom window to escape my dear fiancé, the dullest man I have ever known. I'd spent a good hour listening to him rehearsing a sermon—he was a clergyman you see—but I was simply driven to leave. I didn't actually choose him you know. My mother did. Of course he was mortally offended but I made up my mind there and then he'd never get me to the altar so I broke off the engagement. Broke my mother's heart, so she said. I don't think I'd have made a good vicar's wife in any case, I actually like to speak my mind. The high point in my life was travelling the world before I finally settled in these wondrous, alluring tropics. I crave the heat and the colour."

"You're English Miss Forsyth," Jude said. Miss Forsyth still retained what Jimmy called her "hoity-toity" accent.

"Anglo-Irish family," she corrected. "I always thought

Lester Rogan had more than a hint of an Irish accent hidden away there,'' she mused with a frown. ''He was at pains to get rid of it for some reason. In my opinion he exaggerated his Australian drawl.''

"That's true," Cate considered, on reflection. "He had two voices actually. I'd forgotten about that."

"He had two personalities more like it," Jimmy crowed.

"Is it possible Ireland was his homeland?" Jude put the question to Miss Forsyth.

"He claimed he'd lived in Australia all his life, that he was born here," she answered giving it frowning consideration.

"But you doubted that?"

"As I said, there was something about his accent if one listened carefully. It was a hybrid. In later years he favoured what is known as ocker but he didn't speak like that in the early days."

"Cate's father was Irish." Jude shot a glance at Miss Forsyth, studying Cate's face along the way.

"Yes, I know."

"Could it be Cate's father and Lester Rogan were somehow connected? Related perhaps?"

Cate flared. "Even if that were true, which it isn't, why would Lester Rogan leave me a fortune simply on the strength of a distant relationship?"

"Who said distant, Cate? This is an important avenue that has to be checked out."

"He didn't leave a letter, Jude, to explain his actions?" Miss Forsyth asked. "One might have thought so. Dear Matthew would surely have persuaded him?"

"No letter." Jude shook his head, his eyes still on Cate's troubled expression. "I've been right through Dad's files, but I can double-check."

"Matty would have known of the connection surely?"

Jimmy said. "Les would have confided in him, he told ya dad things he told no on else. Course no one was to know ya dad would die so early."

"Indeed, yes," said Miss Forsyth. "A tragedy! Really Lester put everyone in a terrible position," she shook her snowy head ruefully. "Look at poor Cate, I dread to think what might have happened to her had you not arrived last night, Jude."

Jude's eyes were a blue blaze. "I couldn't force Cate to make a complaint but I can talk to Ralph. And his mother."

"Poor Myra has no control over Ralph," Miss Forsyth said with authority. "Parents can be as big a disappointment to their children as children are to their parents. Myra has absolutely no force of character and, as a result, Lester walked all over her. Never did love her, you know, poor little thing. She was just another piece of property he snaffled up. Married her because he thought it would be the smart thing to do. His father-in-law taught him everything about the real estate business, property development. Lester's rise was meteoric."

"Sure was!" Jimmy exclaimed. "He started to make it big only a couple of years after he married Myra. Not that he didn't have a fair bit of his own money. Where did he get that, I wonder? Basically he was a bit of a larrikin I always thought. Not a gentleman like ya dad, Jude. If only you had your dad to talk to, he could tell you all we need to know."

CHAPTER SEVEN

JUDE found Ralph sitting behind his father's desk in the study of the Rogan mansion. He hadn't rung ahead to say he was coming. That would have given Ralph the opportunity to takeoff. Melinda had let him into the house, her small pretty face alight with pleasure. Now she stood at the door of the study, obviously wanting to be part of whatever discussion was about to take place only her brother barked at her.

"All right, Mel. No need to hang around. You can go. Jude wants to talk to me, not you."

Jude looked at Melinda with a sympathetic smile. "I'll see you before I leave, Mel. What I have to say is for Ralph's ears. How's your mother?"

"Doing what she always does," Ralph exploded. "Lying down. You'd think she was the only woman in the world who'd lost a husband. Not a loving husband who was damned good to her, either. A real bastard."

"How can you talk like that, Ralph?" his sister protested, her fair skin turning beet red. "You must have hated Dad."

"Fact is you did, too, Mel. Why don't you grow up? Get yourself a job. There must be something you wanna do?"

"Have you got to be so offensive, Ralph?" Jude protested, mouth tightening. "Or are you going to spend the rest of your life injuring your mother's and your sister's psyches. Haven't they had enough of that? Haven't you?"

"Maybe I'm more like my rotten father than I thought," Ralph sighed, suddenly sounding sad.

"You don't have to follow the very same course. You

can change, Ralph. You can commit to shrugging off the past and looking towards the future. As for Mel! She could travel,'' Jude suggested. ''There's a big wide world for you to see, Mel.'' He turned his face to her. ''I'm sure you would benefit greatly from the experience.''

''She'd be too bloody nervous to try,'' Ralph scoffed, not about to change overnight. ''She'd rather stay home and lead the same old miserable life.''

''And it must be as miserable as it gets, with you for a brother,'' Jude said. ''If I were you, Ralph, I'd have a care how I spoke to my mother and sister. This isn't your house. This isn't your study and that isn't your chair. The house belongs to your mother.''

''That's right, Ralph,'' Melinda piped up, looking as though she hadn't realised that fact until it was confirmed by Jude. ''Mum could throw you out.''

''Don't make me laugh.'' There was a malicious glint in Ralph's eyes. ''Mum doesn't understand a thing about anything, even running this house.''

''She can find out,'' Jude retorted. ''She can hire a house manager, start with a housekeeper. All these things are easily attended to. I'll find her someone to help her manage her financial affairs, Mel, too, if that's what she wants. I'm here to help.''

''Of course you are.'' Ralph rocked back in his late father's custom made leather chair. ''You're the man. The knight in shining armour.''

''Trust me,'' Jude's blue eyes blazed. ''I'm here to look after your mother's and sister's interests, that goes for Cate Costello as well. Would you like to tell Mel what you got up to last night before I tell the whole town?''

Ralph's mouth fell slightly ajar. ''You wouldn't dare.''

''Don't be ridiculous,'' Jude looked at him with contempt.

"What did he do?" Melinda ventured timidly into the room, pulling at the fingers of her right hand.

"Can you understand plain English?" her brother shouted in frustration. "This has got nothing to do with you, Mel."

"It might be best if you go, Mel," Jude advised. "You've enough grief in your life."

Melinda stood motionless for a moment, staring at her brother. "One day you're going to do something really horrible, Ralph."

"If you're not careful I'll do it right now." Her brother stumbled to his feet.

"Sit down, Ralph and don't move," Jude said in such a way Ralph found himself doing it. "You're in enough trouble as it is."

"Could I get you something, Jude?" Melinda asked. "Tea, coffee a cold drink?" She cocked her head, rather like a bird.

Jude felt his heart ache for her. What a hell of an upbringing both Mel and Ralph had had. "I'm fine for the moment thanks, Mel. We might have a cup of coffee together before I go."

"Lovely!" Burning spots of colour went straight to Mclinda's cheeks.

"She fancies herself in love with you, silly little twit," Ralph told Jude after his sister had left the room, closing the door behind her.

"Nonsense!" Jude brushed that off. "Exactly how often does Mel see me?"

Ralph ignored that. "Yeah, well, if you don't want to listen. Poor old Mel has had the hots for you since we were kids. Even I know that's not your fault, part of Mel's problem is she's only good for daydreams. Plus you're the sort of guy who takes a woman's breath away. Isn't that right? Even up here we get the papers."

Jude shrugged. "That was probably the dumbest article ever published, but I haven't come here to chat about me. I really want to talk about you and your recent activities."

"Uh-huh," said Ralph, rocking back, his hands behind his head. "I know I didn't handle myself well last night but I did apologise. I was drunk. Up to my ears in booze. I—"

"And you came back." Jude cut him off. "You ransacked her flat?"

"No way!" Ralph looked the very picture of innocence. "You're off your trolley."

"I don't think so. Your DNA is all over the place."

"So what?" Ralph curled his lip. "I've admitted to calling in on the conniving little bitch."

"I won't listen to your calling her names, Ralph," Jude warned, pulling up an armchair to the desk.

"Oh dear, got you in as well has she?" Ralph hunched his broad shoulders. "I guess she's beautiful if you like the type. I don't. After I left you I drove over to Amy Gibson's place where I crawled into her bed. Ring Amy if you like, she'll vouch for my whereabouts," Ralph added in triumph.

"So what do you have to buy her?" Jude asked. "Only a fool would believe you. You had opportunity and motive, also you get people to do things on your behalf. The police will be asking you more questions, Ralph." Given Cate's refusal that simply wasn't true, but Jude allowed it to pass in the hope it might catch Ralph out.

"Yeah, well, they won't put me at the scene," Ralph countered aggressively. "Someone else had to tear the place to pieces. Not me. A lot of guys in town are mighty interested in her. Maybe she sucked a guy in then told him to get lost. She sure turned her attention on Dad and look where it got her. The old goat was her lover."

Ghastly thought. "I know different, Ralph," Jude said, thinking such a discovery would affect him drastically. "Go near her again, threaten her or her property in any way and you do it at your peril. I mean that. I'll fix you and I'll fix it you wind up in court. Courts take a very dim view of stalking and harassment. You always were a bully."

Ralph was looking wary now. "For hell's sake, aren't we suppose to be working together? That girl, that redheaded bitch, has stolen my inheritance. I'm the rightful heir. The only son. Who the hell is she? If she wasn't his mistress, what else? Just because she looks so angelic doesn't mean she didn't work frantically to ingratiate herself with my fool of an old man."

"Except no one in the world would agree with that description of your father." Jude pointed out very dryly.

"He did come to fancy classy little chicks. Little chicks with big green eyes and long silky hair."

Jude shook his head with emphasis. "I might have agreed with you for about five minutes, Ralph, but not now. There's a story behind all this."

"Of course there's a story!" Ralph exploded. "There has to be. Is it possible she's his byblow? He had countless affairs in his life. Half the time Mum never knew where he was."

Jude knew that to be completely true. "I promise you I'll carry out an investigation and report back to you. In the meantime, Ralph, I'm here to deliver a warning. Keep off the grog and keep away from Cate Costello."

Ralph still looked like he was slightly drunk. He hadn't shaved, a couple of days dark growth on his cheeks and chin. "You two are getting pretty close, aren't you?" he asked in a snide voice. "Anyway what does it all matter?" Abruptly he lost all aggression, sounding depressed." How are you going to fix it? I can't possibly sit still and let a total stranger get away with family money. I know you wouldn't. You'd fight like hell, don't tell me you wouldn't. The whole thing's crazy.''

Jude nodded. ''I agree. So does Cate Costello I'd have you know. She swears she had absolutely no idea why your father would do such a thing.''

Ralph swore violently and waved his arms in the air. ''Who would trust a woman? Would you, Jude? Didn't your mum do a real wicked thing without warning. She ran off with some Yank. Left you and your dad to fend for yourselves. That's women for you,'' Ralph swore again.

''It's not sex they're after. It's money. Lots of it. It's always been the same. They sell their bodies on the street. They sell them in swank hotels. Prostitutes. Society women. It's money they're after the same way men go after power. What's she doing up here anyway? Hell, she could have followed Dad up here. Ever thought of that? Maybe she was Mandel's little girlfriend at one time. Attractive bloke, Tony, even if he was old enough to be her father. Maybe Mandel leaked news of a filthy rich property developer up in Isis with an eye for the ladies. Who knows?'' Ralph's dark eyes looked tragic.

''There's another angle, Ralph,'' Jude said. ''Did your father ever speak of his childhood, where he was born? Did he have family?''

Ralph stared back, rubbing his hand over the dark stubble on his face. ''Struth I'll have to have a shave! I tell you I feel stripped of my inheritance, by a total stranger. I was the heir apparent. Now look what it's come to. As for Dad! We'd all have gone into shock if he'd ever confided in us about anything. He was the kinda guy who left everyone wondering. He told Mum once before they married he lost his whole family when he was young. I'm not sure now he didn't kill 'em, or maybe he just wished them all dead. I can't tell you anything about my father's background. He's one of those people who just appears out of nowhere.''

''There are ways to get information. Miss Forsyth detected the hint of an Irish accent or inflection tucked away there?''

Ralph gave an acrid laugh. ''How the hell would she know?''

''She came from an Anglo-Irish family.''

''She's a Pom. I thought she was smart but she must be a bit stupid after all. Dad's accent was pure Ocker. What has Irish got to do with it anyway?''

''Cate Costello's father was born in Ireland. He died some years back so we can't speak to him.''

''About what?'' There was genuine confusion in Ralph's handsome beefy face.

''About some possible link, Ralph. We need some answers. I don't blame you or your family for feeling betrayed, I do blame you however for your attack on Cate Costello. I'm convinced she's the innocent victim in all this.''

''Victim?'' Ralph hooted. ''She's rich! Big-time rich!''

''There are circumstances here we don't know about. I'm asking you to give me a little time.''

Ralph shifted back and forth in the huge armchair. ''Aren't you going back to your city job?''

Jude shook his head. ''I'm not going anywhere for a while, I'm on vacation. That should be time enough.''

Ralph looked like he was hurting badly. ''I'm not going to let her get away with this, Jude,'' he warned. ''I can't live with what Dad's done. He owed me.''

Jude gave him a long straight look. ''Legally he didn't owe you anything, Ralph. As it is you inherited a tidy sum. Most people don't see that kind of money in a lifetime. I know it's nowhere near what you expected.''

'I'm not going to be defeated,'' Ralph said. ''She's not

the pure little thing she's pretending. She could be treacherous. Men lose themselves in a woman's face, we're like little boys when we want them but it takes time to find out about their hearts. You should know that, Jude.

"Find out about her." Ralph went on earnestly. "We've never been friends. I can never learn to like you. Not after the way my dad held you up to me as a role model. I was never smart or special enough, but you were, and your father loved you, you needed each other. Dad didn't need us. Strangely enough I'm clear on one thing, I trust you as a man. I trust you as a lawyer, executor of my father's estate. Find out about her, Jude. Find out what she's been up to. If we learn the real truth about her, we might be able to cut a deal."

Jude stood up. "Don't forget I've got a deal for you as well. Who knows what you planned when you called on Cate early in the evening. She thought you meant to attack her. Maybe you didn't ransack her place yourself but we both know you could find someone to do it. Probably Kramer—I bet you told him to wear gloves. There better not be any more attempts to frighten her much less harm her. I could just as easily bash your head in today as I did years ago. I wouldn't want to do that. I dislike violence and I'm a lawyer. Tell your friend, Kramer, I'm pointing a finger at him as well."

"There'll be no trouble," Ralph growled. "Tell that to your little girlfriend. All she's had so far is a protest. You promise me you'll look into it?"

"I have to look into it, Ralph. The key is somewhere in past lives. I'm sure of it."

By the time Jude arrived back at the gallery, the living quarters had been completely restored to order. Late afternoon sunshine spilled through the large picture windows falling on a beautiful arrangement of the sacred blue lotus which grew in abundance in the North. One perfect large open flower was at the lowest level of the tall arrangement, sitting on an open leaf. He could see two buds, two pods, tightly furled leaves and open leaves all displayed in a lotus shaped bronze vase. Cate was bending over it making slight adjustments to the tallest, soaring leaf. He felt the urgency to go to her startling. He'd heard about a coup de foudre. He appeared to have caught it full blast.

She broke off what she was doing the moment she saw him. "How did you go? I've been so worried."

"No need." He walked through the open door, seeking to reassure her. "Ralph was at the house and we had a talk. He as good as admitted he had someone trash the place. It was in the nature of a protest he said, I rather think it won't happen again. I'm pretty sure Ralph didn't do it himself. Like you said he has a girlfriend to vouch for his whereabouts, but he gave the order. That's a beautiful arrangement." He wanted so much to touch her it hurt. "Where did you get the flowers?"

"Jimmy brought them back for me. He knows I like the Japanese Rikka style of flower arrangements. I studied it for a while though to become a master would take a lifetime."

"Well, you've done a pretty good job. That's beautiful."

"Thank you." Her hand caressed a furled bud. "The buds are the hope for the future. You have such exquisite water lilies here in the tropics. The large leaves are so decorative, don't you think? Miss Forsyth actually gave me this pot. It's very old. I love it."

He didn't reply and she sought his eyes. "You're doing rather a lot for me, Jude. Going to see Ralph Rogan. I've seen how dangerous he can be."

He heard the faint tremor in her voice. "Ralph has been warned off. Did you ask Miss Forsyth if you could stay with her for a night or two? I take it Hazlett has finished up here?''

''Only just. It took hours. The alarm emits quite a din. If anyone should try to break in the whole neighbourhood is going to know about it.''

''Good,'' he said with satisfaction.

''I didn't say anything to Miss Forsyth,'' she confessed. ''Actually she asked me if I'd like to spend the night with her. I thanked her and told her I'd be perfectly all right here.''

''Will you?'' He stared into her eyes.'' I was hoping you'd come back and stay with me at least until your nerves settle. Mine, too, for that matter.''

She averted her bright head. ''I can't, Jude.''

''Why not? It's not as though I'm proposing an orgy. Nothing is going to get out of hand. I just want you under my nose until things cool down. We could buy a bottle of wine and some seafood for dinner. We can pick up everything we need for a salad at one of the farms along the way. It's the perfect time for you to tell me all about yourself. I need to know.''

''I don't want to leave the gallery,'' she said, though it cost her an effort.

His blue eyes trapped her. ''We activate the security system. That's what it's all about.''

Cate slowly let the breath in and out of her lungs. Why was she making it so easy for him to sweep her off her feet. Where were the strong defences she'd built to avoid all kinds of grieves?

''Cate,'' he said gently. ''I know you have something to tell me.''

''Hasn't everyone something to tell?''

He shrugged. ''Probably, but your story is more shattering than most. I won't let anything threaten you. No one is going to bother you, that includes me. You've had two bad experiences. Give yourself a little time to get over them.''

''I've had worse experiences,'' she said.

''Maybe it would help to tell someone about them,'' he said very seriously. ''Look at me, Cate.''

For a moment she didn't respond. ''Was it really only yesterday we set eyes on each other?''

''I've no idea,'' He gave her a self-deprecating smile. ''You're a witch. You've cast a spell on me.''

''What kind, though?''

''The mysterious kind,'' he said.

She stared up at him with unreadable intensity. ''Then take every precaution.''

He let his eyes linger on her lovely face. ''Thank you for the warning, Cate. I intend to.''

Jude hand-picked the wine—a multiaward winning sparkling as an aperitif, and a beautiful riesling that would go well with the seafood. The seafood in the Great Barrier Reef waters was plentiful and superb. They bought oysters, prawns, crab and crayfish; fresh rolls and a chocolate and almond strudel that had just come out of the oven at the bakery. Cate said she could make a avocado and papaya salad from what was growing in Jude's backyard. Along the beach road they stopped at a farm to buy lots of freshly picked herbs and salad greens, Jude getting into animated conversation with the owners, a married couple of Italian descent he had known all his life. Cate was introduced, smiled upon warmly, both sent off with much more than they actually paid for.

''Is this a celebration?'' Cate enquired, when they were back on the road again.

''Why not?'' He threw her a lazy grin.

''Please don't say it's because I've come into a fortune.''

"Did I say that?" he retorted.

"No. I know you came here as executor of Lester Rogan's will, Jude, but I'm hoping you're going to be my friend."

"What do you think I've been doing?" he chided her.

"Questioning me whilst being very kind. Observing me while I'm not looking. All the time thinking, is it possible she could have been...?"

"Rogan's mistress? It's a thought that would enter anyone's mind, Cate. Rich men of any age can attract beautiful young women. We all know that. We see it and read about it all the time. It didn't take me long to reach the conclusion there was no relationship."

"Sexual relationship."

"Don't brood about it," he advised. "Minutes ago you were laughing with the Pagliaros."

"They accepted me because I was with you. I wonder if they'd have looked at me differently if they'd known Lester Rogan had left me so much money?"

"Money alone has a certain cachet," he said dryly. "They took to you because you're a beautiful young woman with a poised, friendly manner. I took to you the instant I laid eyes on you. That was in the church when you were trying unsuccessfully to melt into the shadows. I took to you even more when we began talking."

"And now?" She glanced at his handsome profile.

"I told you. You've laid a spell on me." He was silent a moment then added rather sombrely, "Women have such power."

"What are you thinking about right now?" she asked. "Please tell me. What made you look so grim all of a sudden. Is it something about me?"

"Of course not." He sought to reassure her. She sounded slightly unnerved.

"Then what? Are you thinking about the mother you loved?" she asked with great seriousness.

"The truth, Cate?" His eyes were a blue blaze. "I think of her frequently. You'd think with all the years that have passed I'd think of her less and less but it's not working out that way. Neither of my parents have disappeared, they're locked into my mind. They come to me in dreams. Strangely enough they're happy dreams when my mother loved my father and me."

"You've never tried to find her, Jude?" Cate shook her head thinking she couldn't let such a thing happen. For all Jude's natural charm of manner, the blond hair, the blue eyes and that "heartbreaker" smile, she had come to realise he wasn't a man to be trifled with. Not him or his emotions.

"She doesn't want to be found, Cate," he told her tersely. "Otherwise she would have contacted us. She simply walked out of the house and out of our lives."

"Yet she looks so beautiful in her portrait. She looks a loving woman."

"The loving didn't last." His voice held betrayal. "At least not for us."

"That is so, so sad. I know what's it's like to be desperately lonely for a mother's love. That terrible morning, our last morning together, I kissed my mother goodbye. A hurried peck I so regret. I was late for my lift you see. I told her I'd be home late. There was a rehearsal for the school play, Romeo and Juliet. I was Juliet. I was excited about it, I loved acting. When my friend's mother dropped me off late that afternoon she was gone. I rang around everywhere. All her friends. One of our neighbours told me she saw my mother heading off with our dog for a walk in the forest. That was hours before. I got on my bike and rode until it was dark but there was no sign of her or Blaze. When my stepfather came home he rang the police. I never saw her

again. It's truly dreadful when someone just disappears.
There's no coming to grips with it. There is no conclusion.
My stepfather is a monster. I hate him.''

Jude understood from the vehemence in her voice there
was more to tell. Whether he would reach the status of
trusted confidante he didn't yet know.

What am I doing here, Cate thought, unpacking her overnight bag in the welcoming white and yellow guest bedroom
with its touches of blue. This wasn't the sort of thing she
would normally do, yet here she was spending another night
at Jude's home. The sea breeze was blowing the filmy white
draperies at the open French doors so she went to tie them
back with their yellow silk cords. That done, she paused for
long moments to look out at the beautiful ocean front setting
with its profusion of palms and pandanus. In the afternoon
sunlight a golden glitter was coming off the brilliantly blue
water, bordered as it was by mile after mile of pristine-white
sands.

She loved Jude's house. It seemed to her so romantic.
She loved the way all the doors in the house opened out
onto that glorious view. She had lived in far more formal
houses, in a cooler climate but she loved the rather glam-
orous informality and the streaming floods of sunlight.
Many the Sunday afternoon she had driven out to Spirit
Cove just to park near Jude's house and admire it. Jimmy
had told her so much about his friends the Conroys. Father
and son. She had recognised Jude the moment she laid eyes
on him just from Jimmy's description. Jude was certainly
very handsome with an easy effortless charm that could,
however, turn into moments of sombre brooding.

She wasn't scared of him in any way. One only had to
look at Jude to know he wasn't a man who would ever harm
a woman. The truth was she was scared of herself. It was

getting to the stage where he had only to beckon and she would follow. That in itself was extraordinary. Always with admirers and she'd had them, she was the one to back off. She could have found herself a husband a dozen and more times during her time in the Outback.

Out there women were outnumbered by heaps of bush bachelors desperately looking for a wife. Nice guys, too. Manly and caring. One could almost say courtly. Women were a precious commodity and treated as such. Unfortunately, psychologically speaking she was damaged, still caught in a trap of helpless anger and grief. At twenty-two nearly twenty-three she was still unable to cast it off.

Or was that the past? Jude Conroy was handling her very easily. She couldn't bear to think of it as manipulation? In fact the strange bond between them was going ahead in great leaps and bounds. Apart from the strong physical attraction neither of them was able to deny, was it because bad things had happened to them when they were children? Both of them were orphans. Both had suffered the disastrous consequences of having their mothers simply disappear from their lives. Great losses like that changed one's inner landscape.

Successful as Jude had become as a lawyer she knew from the way he spoke a great deal of bitterness, anger and grief continued to hold sway. She wondered if he was involved with someone. He had to be. Women didn't let men like Jude get away. She decided she would ask him. That kiss he had given her on the beach had been so passionate, so shattering, she found it hard to believe he could kiss her like that and be seriously involved with someone else. Or had it been simply associated with the moment? She had been in an overexcited and agitated state. She truly believed she had seen a woman in a long white dress walking on the beach. She still believed it. She would go on believing it even if the whole world put it down to imagination. She had eyes. It was painfully obvious she had a vulnerable heart.

A tap on the door had her spinning her head. "Oh, hi, Jude," she said, trying to smile when she had the sensation her blood was sparkling, rushing, instead of moving calmly through her veins.

"I thought I'd come collect you." He moved across the spacious room to join her, the sun catching the bright honey-blond gloss of his hair.

"I'd fallen into a daydream," she tried to explain. "This cove is an especially beautiful part of the coast. I love your house. I'd love to live here. I'd love to swim morning and evening, go for long walks, work in your beautiful garden. I'd restore the flower beds, tropical flowering is so brilliant it would be an easy task. I love the lemon tropical netting on my tester bed there, the polished floors, the oriental rugs, the furniture, the wicker and rattan and bamboo, all the Thai pieces and the Chinese garden stools. I adore the huge deck. It's a wonderful place for entertaining."

"It's where we're going to have dinner." He smiled, looking into her expressive face.

"Perfect," she sighed.

"So what else would you do with the house?" he asked sounding both pleased and amused.

"It's possible you wouldn't let me do anything. May I ask you a question, Jude?"

"Sure. Fire away." He looked down into her lustrous green eyes.

"Do you have a girlfriend?"

He gave her a slight and dangerous smile. "At the risk of sounding immodest I'm phenomenally popular at the moment."

"Really? And where is the lucky woman? Or is it women?"

"Woman," he said. "She's the senior partner's daughter."

She shied away from that. It made her unsettled and unhappy. "Does she work with you?"

"No, thank goodness!" He reverted to sardonic tones.

The constriction in her chest miraculously lifted. "You mean she's a huntress?"

"Aren't you all?"

"Shame on you, Jude. I'm not hunting you."

"Poppy is." He gave her his heart-catching lopsided smile.

"What does she do?"

"She likes to ambush me in my office," he said dryly.

"But you're a big boy. I would have thought you'd know how to handle yourself."

"It's not as easy as all that, Cate." He shook his head. "I think her father actually approves of me as a son-in-law."

"You don't have your heart set on promotion, a spot of social climbing?" she asked as casually as she could.

"Seriously, Cate, I don't want to lose my job. I've worked very hard to get where I am. I have the feeling Poppy has the potential to turn nasty. She's a girl who only knows about getting what she wants."

"Is she beautiful?" She almost hoped he would tell her this Poppy was plain, but of course she wouldn't be.

"She's a blond bombshell," Jude confirmed her worst fears.

"How very fortunate for you." She brushed a lock of hair out of her eyes.

"And she's irrelevant," he said. "Actually I'm hoping she'll find someone else while I'm away."

"Kissing strange women on the beach?" she countered, bittersweet.

"Well, well, Cate Costello," he said softly, "you sound jealous?" He lifted his hand to tuck flying strands of copper hair behind her ears. "If you must know, ours was a kiss unparalleled until, I guess, the next time."

Sexual desire was exciting. It could also be full of woe. "What do you want from me, Jude?" she asked. There was so much going on between them.

"To spend time with you," he replied." To get to know you, to help you if I can. It sounds like there's been an absence of love in your life."

"I could say the same of you," she said quietly. "You've laid a few of your grieves bare. Are you telling me the truth about Poppy? Have you made love to her?"

"I'd like to hear about your love life," he parried. "I've dated a lot of girls, Cate, but I've never been bewitched until now."

He lifted his hand slowly to place his palm against her cheek, a gesture so tender, so seductive, Cate felt herself dissolve.

"What is it, Cate?" he asked with intensity.

"Surely everything I'm feeling is on my face," she met his eyes.

"I'm aching to kiss you." The tautness of his handsome features gave his longing away. "I've been aching to kiss you all day. Kiss your perfect lips." In a strong movement that revealed the depth of his hunger, he put his arms around her, one hand pressing into her back so he could gather her closer into his body.

It was so overwhelming one part of Cate urged her to pull away before she was lost. She needed to keep control of herself but control was spinning away. She wanted to be wild and free. Her breasts were in urgent contact with his chest. He smelled wonderful. Masculine, fresh, clean, salt, sandalwood, a note of vanilla.

"I'll let you move away if you want to," he muttered. "Only I want you to know I'll take the greatest care of you."

Care? She couldn't keep the sadness at bay. Didn't he know how easy it would be for him to break her heart? Yet her head fell back, flagrantly inviting him to kiss her throat. Her breath was lost as he did so, his lips moving passionately over the creamy arch, up her chin to the corner of her mouth.

Everything was a glorious, hot, sun-filled silence. The sound of the waves breaking on the shore was totally hushed; the loud swish of the palms. They might have been enclosed in a capsule, she flushed and burning, wanting the ecstasy of his holding her, stroking the side of her mouth with his thumb, gently pressing into the flesh.

What need she had! She wanted more than anything to be close to him. He was physically perfect to her. It was as primitive as mate finding mate. Everything was so easy with him. So acceptable to her. She let him caress her, welcoming his touch.

"Let me look at you. You're so beautiful."

She thought she moaned. She must have because his gentleness turned into a kind of delirium, so passionate, so splendid, she was opening up her mouth to accommodate his tongue. Her arms came up to lock tightly around his neck. She was trembling so violently she had to hold on to something. Hold on to him. She had no armour. No protection now. She needed this level of intensity to ease her own desperate aches.

Jude, too, was trying desperately to come up for air. "Oh, Cate!" he breathed into her mouth. He was losing his sense of everything outside of her. Before his driving male need engulfed him he jerked his head back. What must she think of him? He fancied he could feel her body flinching. Or was it simply a fast trembling? "Cate, I'm sorry. Things get so easily out of hand with you. I don't have any excuse. I brought you back here. But I want you to trust me." He caught her chin, turning up her face so he could read her eyes.

"I do trust you!" Her voice was barely audible.

"It's just so unbelievable what's happening!" Still holding her closely Jude stared out over her head, to the blue sea. "Normally I'm so cautious, but you've got through all my defences." The truth was he was perturbed at his own excesses.

"You shouldn't be afraid to care, Jude," she whispered, her green eyes glistening.

"Don't tremble please." He was trying to soothe her, except he had to let her go. "Look what I've done to you," he murmured with regret.

Cate lifted her head. "Jude, I'm not hurt. I wanted you to kiss me. I'm just a little shaky that's all. I haven't been kissed in a long while. And never like that!"

"Why not? You're so beautiful. You could have any man you wanted."

"Oh, yes," she said wearily, "but I don't want one. I don't like men."

He frowned as dark thoughts he'd refused to consider started to gather in his head. "Could that have anything to do with your feelings for your stepfather?"

"Don't let's talk about him," she said emotionally, fighting an impulse to burst into tears. Even the swiftness and hyperarousal of her feelings for Jude was terrifying in its way. "Look, why don't we go for a walk on the beach?" she suggested, trying hard to steady the tremble in her voice. It might help. No talking, no crying, no kissing, no listening to her heart instead of her head. "Tropical sunsets are glorious."

"As you wish." Why the hell, when he was normally so in control, was he allowing his emotions to soar to extremes? It had everything to do with her. At that moment he honestly believed he didn't have enough strength to withstand her. And he was the one who had promised to keep her safe.

This wasn't a good situation. He'd always thought of himself as a self-sufficient person. Cate Costello with her alluring green eyes had stopped that notion dead in its tracks. Or maybe she had brought him back to the real world?

CHAPTER EIGHT

THE DAYS flew for Jude though his intensive enquiries in relation to Lester Rogan's past weren't bearing any fruit. It was as though the man hadn't existed before he arrived in North Queensland. Finally Jude had to consider calling in a good private investigator to help out. He knew the right man, ex-army intelligence.

He'd tried to elicit information from Myra about her late husband, but Myra appeared to have accepted him at face value. If she'd asked questions in the early days of their courtship Lester Rogan had got by telling her absolutely nothing beyond the fact he no longer had family. From Myra's admittedly hazy recollections he had never mentioned Ireland in any context except once to become extremely angry and upset over the death of some famous race horse over there. Myra couldn't remember anything else. A state of affairs not unparalleled in other relationships where husbands managed to lead double lives and have other children tucked away, Jude had found.

Dermot Costello was a lot easier to get a trace on. Jude was able to establish his arrival in Australia, his career as an architect, followed by his stint as an academic, a career which came to an abrupt tragic end in a car crash in which he was a passenger. The Lundberg case proved the easiest of all to research from the newspapers, though what had happened to Mrs Lundberg, Cate's mother, was by far the hardest mystery to crack. It was difficult indeed to see any connection between Cate's parents and Rogan. Harder yet to see any connection to the Lundbergs or Cate's stepfather, a wealthy, influential man who had resumed his distinguished academic career. Cate had never mentioned there had been a first Mrs Lundberg who had died of a rare heart condition a few years into the marriage.

So Lundberg had lost two wives? Tragedies no man should have to endure. Or something more sinister? Highly respected members of the community were still capable of destroying lives. Power and cruelty often went hand in hand. Jude had come to believe Lundberg at some stage must have betrayed an infatuation with Cate. Her aversion to him appeared to have strong sexual overtones.

Cate had spent that second night at his house and then insisted on returning home. He saw her for a short time each day as he saw the Rogan family. There were no more disturbances at the gallery. Ralph had made no further attempt to approach Cate, but Jude knew Ralph was just barely biding his time. He'd even heard from Jimmy Ralph was going around town trying to find evidence of a sharp decline in his father's mental condition; rambling conversations, bad business deals and the like. According to Jimmy who had his ear to the ground, Ralph hadn't yet humiliated himself by telling the town of the disposition of his father's will.

"What he's tryin' to do is find proof his old man was going ga-ga," Jimmy chortled. "He'll have a job on his hands."

That indeed was the question. Was Lester Rogan before his death in full possession of his faculties? Even that question was irrelevant. Lester had had Jude's father draw up a new will naming Cate as his main beneficiary two years previously. Though Jude had searched through every scrap of paper his father had kept on Lester Rogan and his affairs, there remained the possibility his father had stashed a file elsewhere, for safe keeping.

For the time they were apart, Jude pictured Cate back in

his house. He had an excuse to get her there by asking her to help him conduct a search for a possible missing file. If he tried very hard he could keep his mind on the job.

She arrived midmorning of the following Saturday with the glorious weather of the week giving way to an ominous build-up of incandescent storm clouds. Such a display building up over the sea presaged the start of the late afternoon thunderstorms that were so much a feature of the tropics on the verge of the Wet. They were spectacular but short lived.

"Thanks for coming." He allowed himself the luxury of kissing her cheek and caught a drift of her special fragrance. The last thing he wanted to do was frighten her away. He realized there were lots of things Cate was trying to block out. But she leaned towards him, seeming to give a little sigh. Did she know what hope that offered him?"

They walked up the short flight of steps together to the porch. "I think we're in for a storm," she remarked.

"For sure." He surveyed the sky, brilliantly blue over the house, threatening over the ocean.

"Find out anything more?"

"Not much I'm afraid. Lester Rogan might have descended from another planet."

"Maybe Rogan's not his name?" Cate suggested, "Maybe he reinvented himself."

"Very possibly," Jude murmured, ushering her inside. "The big question is why? Like a cold drink? I've actually got some home made lemonade. I had to use up some of the lemons. There's a glut of them."

"Lovely. Where are we going to start?" She looked up at him her glowing copper head tilted to the side.

"Where would you think? Where would my father be likely to hide a document he didn't particularly want anybody to find?"

"The bookcases in the study spring immediately to

mind,'' Cate said, having glimpsed the room the first night. ''My father was always pushing newspaper clippings or scraps of information he wanted to keep in among the books. I saw him do it often.''

Jude considered for a moment. ''My dad didn't do that as far as I can recall, he was strictly methodical. But we can try.''

It was a fairly daunting task. There were legal tomes, countless reference books, books on international law, economics, science, many fields of knowledge other than the law. His father had been interested in so much. History, music, mathematics biographies of famous people mostly nineteenth and twentieth century.

''This is a major undertaking,'' Jude said, leaning back against his father's desk. ''And that doesn't include the innumerable files relating to Dad's clients. I've read everything I can find on Lester Rogan.''

Cate let her eyes roam around the large airy fan cooled room. All the windows and shutters were open, affording a beautiful view of the side garden. ''Your father must have been a very well-read man,'' she commented.

Jude glanced at his father's high-backed leather chair. He fancied he could see his father sitting in it, head bent, poring over some papers. ''He was indeed. Far better read than I'll ever be and far more learned. In many ways he wasted his life here. There was talk of making the shift to Brisbane when I was about ten or eleven. He had connections with various law firms and he was concerned about me and my tertiary education. There was no more talk after my mother took off. He lost all heart. Or what heart he had was for me.''

''You loved him very much?'' she asked, wishing she could ease some of the pain away.

''I did. I do. He was the sort of man who did everything

to help people.'' Jude stared back into her eyes, nearly groaning at their look of tenderness. For him? ''All of which convinces me Dad wouldn't have left you with a huge problem.''

Cate looked away. ''He probably didn't expect to die so early, Jude. Any more than my father. He and a colleague were on their way to a meeting, only they met up with death instead. Surely your father would have asked Lester Rogan about me? Who I was? From all accounts he could handle Lester Rogan.''

''Rogan trusted him.'' Jude nodded. ''They weren't exactly friends, but he did go big game fishing with Dad from time to time.''

''On the face of it, the will isn't fair. I shouldn't inherit over his wife and children.'' Cate insisted.

''Hold on. We haven't solved this yet. Dad must have put the truth of the matter down somewhere. We could have an investigation conducted by a professional but it could take much longer than you think. The big problem is we don't have much time. Ralph has a short fuse.''

''At least he hasn't come near me.'' Cate couldn't control a shiver. ''We'd better make a start.''

His mouth curved into that lopsided smile. A smile that bombarded her senses. ''Which means I might keep you here forever,'' he warned.

She reached out and gently touched his cheek. Sharp, sweet sensations. ''I could make it through dinner.''

''Catherine. Cate. That sounds very provocative?''

''I've missed you,'' she merely said and turned away.

Cate chose one end of the floor to ceiling bookcase which occupied an entire wall of what was a large room. Jude started at the other, running his hand across the spines of the law books that filled the shelves.

By midafternoon despite an exhaustive search they'd found nothing. "I'll make coffee," Jude offered.

"Fine." Cate only nodded. This whole business of her inheritance was beyond her. There had to be some documentation to explain why Lester Rogan had done what he'd done. Her back ached a little but her resolve was firm. She pulled out a leather-bound volume on the voyages of Matthew Flinders, checking there was nothing between the pages.

On the opposite side of the room a dozen or so clients' files fell to the floor with such a clatter it gave her a start. Probably they'd been dislodged by Jude earlier. Her natural reaction was to pick them up and return them to the shelf. It was only when she was shoving them back she realised a wad of what looked like newspaper clippings had stuck to the back wall.

Cate reached for the roll as though it had a special message for her.

"Sick of it?" Jude turned his head to ask as Cate walked into the kitchen. "Cate?" His smile disappeared at the expression on her face. "What is it? You've found something?"

She shook her head from side to side as though she couldn't make sense of anything. Then she passed him what she had in her hand.

"Newspapers clippings!" Jude frowned. There was utter silence while he read them. "What does this mean?" He looked up at her, his blue eyes disturbed.

"It means your father knew all about my mother's disappearance. He kept the clippings, didn't destroy them." She brought her hand to her trembling lips.

"But what does that prove, Cate? My father was interested in all sorts of things. Your mother's disappearance was national news.''

She moved closer, upset darkening her eyes to emerald. ''Do you think he could have known her?''

Jude lifted his wide shoulders, swallowed on the hard knot in his throat. ''I can't see how.''

''Why did he bother to cut all this out?'' She stared at him with those huge, helpless eyes.

''At the moment, Cate, I don't have any idea about anything.'' He kept his voice calm. ''My father wouldn't have hurt a fly.''

''Maybe, but he was helping a man just about everyone hated. Lester Rogan. Could Rogan have known my mother?''

Jude was seriously jolted. ''Or could Rogan have known Lundberg? Though what motive he'd have for getting involved with your stepfather I can't imagine.''

''Let's look some more,'' she urged tautly, already turning back to the study.

Jude followed her, coffee forgotten. ''Where did you find them?''

''Over there.'' She pointed. ''Your father did stuff things into bookcases after all. The files almost jumped off the shelf.'' She indicated which ones.

''And the clippings were behind them?''

''Rolled into a tight wad.''

''Okay, so we shift them all,'' Jude decided, his expression grim.

Jimmy found them some thirty minutes later. ''What's goin' on here?'' he asked in some wonderment.

Neither responded immediately. Finally Jude said, ''You can help, Jimmy. We're trying to find some documentation, some written evidence of the connection between Rogan and

Cate." He didn't mention the newspaper clippings. He knew now Cate hadn't told anyone apart from him her mother's tragic story.

"Right. What are we looking for? Something shoved into or behind a book. Is that it? 'Struth, we'll be here for a month of Sundays. Matty had a book on everything. Where do you want me to start? It's like looking for a needle in a haystack. I bought you a little present by the way, Jude. Thought you could put it up on the wall."

Jude tried to listen to his friend, but felt too stressed. "Thanks, Jimmy," he said absently.

"Aren't you gonna ask me what it is? Hang on a minute, I'll get it. Left it in the hall. Thought you should have it."

He returned in a few moments carrying what looked like a small painting wrapped in bubble paper. "I don't know how long I've had this, but I reckon it's rightly yours."

"Thanks Jimmy," Jude repeated.

"Well open it, son. The big search can wait a minute."

"I'm sorry, Jimmy," Jude stretched his long arms above his head. "This is infuriating. We've established Dad knew who Cate was."

"So who am I?" Cate asked emotionally.

Jimmy went to her, patting her shoulder. "Settle down, love. What's the matter? You can tell Jimmy."

"I don't think I can face what this is all about," Cate said.

"We'll all face it together," Jimmy said. "What do you think, son?" He shot Jude, who was studying his gift, a glance full of affection.

Jude was slow to answer. "I really appreciate this, Jimmy."

"Then that makes me happy," Jimmy said quietly. "Reckon we can find a place for it. Maybe over there?"

He pointed to a section on one wall where a small collection of framed photographs hung.

"Let's do it," said Jude. "Go on helping Cate while I find the hammer and a hook."

"May I see it?" Cate asked after Jude had left the room.

"Of course, love." Jimmy gave her his big affable grin. "It's just a photograph of Matty and his mates on board *Calypso*. Matty was a great big game fisherman. Yours truly is in it too. Good old Lester, another bloke, his friend, and a visiting American film star who was crazy about fishing our Reef waters. We took him out whenever he blew into town." Jimmy picked up the framed photograph, an enlarged glossy from a Cairns newspaper and passed it to her. "Those were the days!"

"You go back a long way, Jimmy," Cate smiled.

She looked down at the photograph. It was then she lost her breath. "Ah, Jimmy!" she moaned, putting the photograph down quickly as though the ebony frame burned her. Bone white she moved into an armchair, lowering her head over her knees.

Jimmy stared at her, shocked. "Catey, what is it? Are you feeling faint, love?"

No response from Cate. She just kept her head down.

Jude coming back into the room reacted swiftly. He went to Cate dropping to his haunches and throwing Jimmy an order over his shoulder. "Get her a drink of water."

"Right, son." Jimmy took off.

"We've been too long at it, Cate. I'm sorry." Compulsively his hand found her nape, soothing, steadying. "This has all been too much for you."

Jimmy returned with a glass of water, putting it into Jude's outstretched hand. "Drink some of this, Cate." Jude raised the glass to her lips.

"I don't think I can swallow."

"Try." He held the glass while she drank from it. "Why don't you lie down on the sofa for a while."

"Yes, love," Jimmy chimed in. "You look awfully white."

Cate let her head fall back against the leather armchair. The tip of her tongue drew beads of water from her lips into her mouth. "The man in the photograph, the man standing next to Lester Rogan is my father." She shut her eyes briefly as if for strength.

Jude stared at her, his heart doing a tumble. "So that's our connection!" He expelled a long breath.

"You're certain, love?" Jimmy turned back to the desktop to reexamine the photograph.

"As certain as I am of my own face."

Jimmy whistled through his nose. "Ya dad, what was he called, love? What was his name? I've never met anyone outside you, called Costello. What was his Christian name? We probably only got around to Christian names."

"Dermot," Cate said, sounding ineffably sad.

Jimmy shook his head. "Never heard that, either. What about Derry?" Jimmy's voice had a questioning inflection. "Now Derry I've heard. I seem to remember Lester acted as though he'd know this Derry all his life. Only Derry was posh. Spoke very correct like Gwennie whereas Lester was anything but. Yet they were friends. Only time I ever saw him, though. Never again."

Jude who had been sitting on the floor at Cate's feet, lifted himself upright. "Feel a little better, Cate?" he eyed her with concern. This rush of information was startling to him let alone her. There was little colour in her lovely skin. "The shocks are coming a bit too thick and fast, aren't they? But we do have a lead. We know of a connection between Lester and your father. I think the answer lies back in

Ireland. Back in their past, Cate. Your father's family could prove to be our best link.''

Cate struggled to clear her head in a terror of confusion. ''I don't know my father's family, Jude. It would be difficult to try to speak to them if my father couldn't. He left home. He travelled as a young man to the other side of the world. Doesn't that say something to you? It was because he could no longer live in his own world. If Jimmy gained the impression Lester Rogan had known my father all his life that means they both lived in the same town or the same district.''

''One was a gentleman. One surely wasn't,'' Jimmy said slowly, measuring every word. ''It's a start. I remember your dad being very good-looking in the Pommy way—I know now he was Irish but I thought then he was English, the skin, you know. Kinda languid if you know what I mean. Maybe graceful is a better word. Not tough like Lester. You can see it right here, the difference in the two men.'' Jimmy tapped a finger at the glass covering the photograph. ''Lester came up real hard, I'd say. Ya dad didn't. But somehow they were bonded.'' Jimmy turned his full attention on Cate. ''Don't you find it amazin' I should bring this photograph over today? I've had it hangin' on my wall for thirty years.''

''I wonder if Myra could remember back that far?'' Jude asked thoughtfully.

Jimmy shook his head. ''Poor Myra has trouble rememberin' what went on yesterday. They weren't livin' together at the time. I mean they weren't married. She could remember somethin' I suppose. Ya dad couldn't have been at the weddin', Cate. Gwennie went and she'd remember the name, Costello. Trust me, Gwennie forgets nuthin'.''

Cate's eyes sought Jude's across the room. ''I think this will get worse, not better,'' she said.

CHAPTER NINE

THE STORM held off until around five-thirty. Jimmy had left an hour earlier to escape it, as great silver laced cumulus clouds raced over the sea like a tidal wave. Soon after Jude had shifted Cate's car into the double garage in case hail attended it.

"I think we'd better close the shutters," he advised with an experienced glance at the now livid sky. Menacing streaks of green and purple rent the billowing grape masses while great gusts of wind gathering force whipped up the white caps on the rolling waves and sent them crashing onto the shore. In the garden and on the strand the fronds of the towering palms were tossed around like silk ribbons. The birds, the brilliantly enamelled parrots, the rose-pink galahs and the beautiful little emerald lorikeets crowned with red, blue, yellow and purple screeched loudly as they winged for shelter in the monumental mango trees that grew in the back garden.

A peculiar fragrance like burning incense hung on the air.

"Not nervous, are you?" Jude asked. Cate was staring fixedly at the lurid sky.

"No, but I haven't seen a sky like that before."

He laughed. "You haven't been here long enough. Tropical storms are volcanic but brief. It's the cyclones you have to watch out for. Better go in, Cate. It's going to come down in a moment."

With the shutters closed one inside of the house was surprisingly dark. She went around turning on a few lights but when Jude came in from the front verandah where he'd been stacking chairs away, he started turning them off. "It won't be for long, Cate," he assured her. "It's an electrical storm, best if they're off. You know not to touch the telephone or the T.V. turn off your computer. Don't stand too near windows and doors." Even as he spoke the remaining light dramatically dimmed.

"It's coming in from the sea, but we can pull the curtain back. It will lighten the room. The awning over the deck is excellent protection but we'll have to keep the doors shut. It'll get hot, but no help for it!"

"It looks dangerous out there," she said, a hand to her throat. "I wouldn't want to be out on a boat." The minute she said it she felt a lurch of dismay. She turned to him her face showing her distress. "I'm so sorry, Jude, I forgot." Too late she remembered Jude's father had been lost at sea.

"Dad died doing what he loved," he said simply. "He wasn't frightened of storms, but he had a proper respect for the sea. I used to love to go out on the boat with him. Took Calypso out myself often enough. Jimmy might have been lost too had he gone with Dad that day."

"The element of chance," Cate said. "Who would have thought Jimmy would choose today to present you with that photograph? If he hadn't, we might never have known my father had been in this part of the world, let alone met your father. It's all incredible to me. I feel it's not real, but a dream."

"It's real enough," Jude said. "We're getting to the truth. The key to Rogan's will lies in the past."

"But that isn't going to satisfy Ralph and his family?"

"No, it won't. I know you find it disturbing but I suppose it's possible Rogan and your father were related? I think the mystery surrounding your mother's disappearance confused us. I don't think there's any connection there. That's an altogether different issue."

"One that desperately needs closure," Cate said. "I pray one day the truth will come out."

"I hope so too, Cate," Jude replied gravely. For the first time it came into his mind he should do something about finding his own mother. She could reject him again, reopen old wounds, but Cate's tragic story made him suddenly think it was worth a try.

"Maybe my father and Rogan were both outcasts?" Cate was saying, her arms folded around her body as she stared out at the storm. "Each in their own way condemned to leave their families behind. The world can be a pitiless place."

"Natures get distorted in the absence of love," Jude said, knowing it to be true.

He walked to where she stood, wanting to rock her like a baby in his arms. It was much too late to banish Cate Costello from his life. The decision was made when he first laid eyes on her. "We can watch the storm together," he said in a quiet voice.

"Put your arms around me," she asked, without looking at him. Waves of excitement were mounting in her, shooting off like so many Roman candles.

"Cate you know where this could lead to," he said into her hair. "You're far too beautiful for me to resist."

"I want to forget everything for a little while."

"Is that the only reason?" He turned her to look at him.

"Sex can be very liberating." There was more than a hint of bravado in her tone.

"I asked if that was the only reason?"

Her expression changed. "You know it isn't." She leaned forward, letting her head rest against his chest. "I trust you, Jude. Something about you speaks to me directly. I'm going to tell you something I've never spoken to anyone about. I felt somehow I'd be exposing my mother and I lived to protect her. For about a year before my mother went missing I had to endure the most excruciating sexual attention from my stepfather.''

Though he had begun to suspect something of the kind he had to brace himself against the shock. ''He surely didn't—?'' He couldn't seem to get his tongue around the word. Not Cate. He put his hand beneath her chin, made her met his eyes.

Cate sighed deeply. ''No. I'd be locked up in a prison if he'd tried that. Only once did he actually grab me, kissing me, fondling my breasts. I nearly fainted from the shock. It was horrible. Demeaning. A frightening experience. My mother wasn't home, she was at a committee meeting. I reacted like a wild thing kicking out. I let him know I'd tell all his colleagues at the university. I'd tell Deborah. I'd tell everyone. Never once did I say I'd tell my mother.''

Jude took her shaking hand, kissed it. ''Because you didn't want to hurt her.''

She inhaled deeply, fighting for control. ''I found it astounding right from the beginning that she was attracted to him. But she must have loved him. Why else would she have married him?''

''Maybe she was the sort of woman who needed a man to take care of her. She had a daughter to rear.''

''It was my fault,'' Cate tightened her arms around her body. ''He told me he married my mother because of me. Can you imagine how that made me feel? It was my fault my mother married him. My fault!''

There was moaning heartbreak in her voice. Outside the deck lit up in a lightning flash. ''You surely can't believe that, Cate. You are not to blame in any way. Your stepfather was sick.''

She laughed bitterly, bending her head forward so her hair screened her face. ''No one we knew would ever have accepted that. I think Deborah became suspicious of him in time.''

''What about your mother? Her maternal instincts? Are you sure she had no inkling of the true nature of his feelings for you? What a terrible problem it presented?''

''She would have had to leave. She did leave.''

''She couldn't have done it deliberately if she loved you.'' Deeply concerned for her, Jude argued strenuously.

Cate looked at him with great brooding eyes. ''No, she didn't.''

''Did you tell the police any of this?''

She shook her head. ''It was a dilemma. I was too ashamed. I raved on about what a Jekyll and Hyde he was but I never said anything about his...touching me. I loved my mother so much I didn't want to tarnish her name. Oh, Jude, can't you understand? I was all mixed up. A schoolgirl.''

''Of course I understand. Could you tell the police now?'' He stared at her gravely.

She reached up to touch his cheek. ''If you were right beside me. You make me feel so much better. Back then I knew I had to keep extremely quiet about what he did. I feared him. He has a marvellous talent for making people believe whatever he says. He was so convincing and he's very rich—people respect money as though that makes you a good person. He thought with my mother out of the way he could turn me into anything he wanted. I was his stepdaughter. He acted as though I belonged to him.''

''So it was one long nightmare?'' Jude asked grimly.

''Hell was more like it.''

''But you had the courage to get away.''

She looked as though she had no courage left. ''Now I'm in another unbearable position. I don't want Lester Rogan's money, Jude.'' There was a slash of colour in her cheeks.

"His family can have it back. As a lawyer you know what to do. I can deed it back to them or whatever. I don't even want to know what link there was between my father and Lester Rogan. If the truth was acceptable it would have surfaced by now. I always sensed Lester Rogan's interest in me wasn't normal."

He picked up on that sharply. "You've never said that before, Cate."

"It wasn't sexual," she was aware of the censure in his voice. "I'm certain of that."

"Even so, you should have said something."

"Maybe you should consider I don't know how to answer questions." She moved closer to the French doors. "Since I lost my father I've led a scary life. Lundberg wisked my mother off. It was like she was the object of a campaign only the campaign was me. My mother and I were enslaved by her marriage to him. She deferred to him on everything like he was some god. He was Professor Lundberg you know. So clever! I was suffocated by his interest in me. What you see, Jude, is the result, I'm sorry if you're disappointed. I'm tired of it all. In coming up here I thought I'd left the past behind, only it has followed me. I'm condemned to relive it."

Her words, so low and rapid, were almost lost to him as the wind screamed across the deck.

He went to her determinedly, drawing her away from the glass doors. Forked lightning sizzled through the dark clouds, creating a beautiful deadly pattern, before it lit up sea and sky in its blinding radiance. Thunder followed, rolling then cracking like a massive military bombardment. Cate literally jumped and he put his arm around her seeing them both reflected in the smoky glass. She looked a white skinned fragile creature beside him.

The wind tore at every door and window, seemingly hell-bent on getting in. Jude felt his own nerves very finely balanced. It had little to do with the storm. He had lived through countless storms and a few spectacular cyclones but the powerful stirrings in his flesh were all caused by a girl who'd had her adolescence stolen from her.

The rain came down. At first a few giant spatters that resounded like artillery on the corrugated iron roof, then a deluge. Silver sheets of water that put the guttering under tremendous pressure.

"This is barbaric!" she whispered in awed fascination, turning her face momentarily against his shoulder as a great jagged fork of lightning slashed down the sky. It illuminated the beach where the vision of a woman in a long white dress was said to appear and disappear in a luminous mist.

He could feel the trembling right through Cate's body. He put his arms around her holding her close to him while the storm screamed around the house seeking entry. A massive clap of thunder that banged the shutters made her gasp. She lifted her face to him, a touch of hysteria in her green eyes.

"That was close."

"Storms frighten you."

"That clap of thunder was like the end of the world." She stared up at him marvelling that he, on the other hand, looked extraordinarily vital. His hair in the rain was a mass of golden ringlets, clinging to his handsome skull.

Her gaze communicated a strange desolation to Jude as if she were renouncing something. Him? He couldn't let that happen. He couldn't let her get away.

With one hand he grasped her long silky hair, the ache so bad, he lowered his head to kiss her. Softly, softly, her lovely mouth parting under the weight of his desire. The intimacy between them had developed at such velocity he thought he'd been waiting for her all his life. For all the convulsive excitements he felt he had to remain mindful of the traumas she'd suffered. His inner voice listened intently to the signals coming off her.

He continued to hold her, a groan coming up from the back of his throat as he pressed kisses all over the face, her throat, her small delicate lobes, murmuring to her all the while, keeping his tone soothing, his touch fluid, drifting lightly over her shoulders to the upper curves of her breasts revealed by the jade camisole she was wearing. Though his own needs were driving he sought to keep them under control. He wanted only what she wanted. To use the slightest force would be to betray her. That would break him to pieces. She had suffered enough.

But she was moaning under his kisses, the slow movement of his hands, the urgent little cries muted by his mouth. Around them was the voice of thunder; the tumultuous sound of the rain drumming on the roof, causing the guttering to overflow, pouring water onto the deck.

The open-mouthed kisses continued, his hand pressing into the back of her head, she was so beautiful! He pulled her in tighter.

After a while, how long?, she seemed to sink against him as if her legs could no longer support her. It was then he lifted her, the whole fragile weight of her, carrying her to the long sofa, still with his mouth at her creamy throat. He sank to his knees while she lay there, one arm flung above her head, he trying to beat back overwhelming desire. It must have shown in his face because she put trembling fingers to the buttons of his shirt, slipping them one by one, allowing her hand to move across his chest. That small cool hand burned.

He could hear the heavy thud of his heart as his mouth dipped to hers. This time he crushed it because he couldn't keep the extreme gentleness up. His passion was too fierce. It overflowed.

"I have to see you, look at you." His voice sounded slurred. He was drunk on her beauty. Her green eyes clung to his as he pushed the narrow straps of her camisole top off her shoulders. She was wearing a strapless bra with lace cups beneath. In an ecstasy of longing he bowed his head to suckle each erect nipple that showed duskily through the delicate material, now damp from his mouth.

Finally, because he was driven to, he lifted her upper body slightly so he could release the hook. Then he took her naked breasts into his hands holding like they were the sweetest of fruit.

I've fallen in love, Cate thought. Me who has hidden from love for a long time. She had never known such tenderness, such exquisite delicacy from a man's strong hands. He was peeling the clothes from her as he might peel a peach, slowly, gently, giving her time to stay him if she wanted, but she had entered a zone of physical rapture.

An extraordinary thing was happening to her. With her eyes tightly closed she felt his hands begin to explore her body, the silken, supple, yielding flesh. She could feel the faint tremble in his warm fingers as though he found her utterly beautiful.

So this was what falling in love was like? Only a lover could demolish the strong defences she'd taken refuge behind.

"Cate?"

She had to clutch at him, every nerve rippling, electric.

"I hear you." Slowly she opened her eyes on his taut handsome face, feeling the heat rise from her skin.

"I want to take you to bed." He watched her intently with those blazing blue eyes. "I want to make love to you properly. I have protection."

"You can't protect me from you." She lifted an arm to encircle his neck, her fingers spearing in to those crisp golden curls. "I knew what would happen when I said I'd stay." She smiled at him, a smile of deep significance for Jude.

It held trust and something equally as powerful. Pure desire. He put his arms beneath her, gathering her up as though she was the most precious of creatures. "You're sure?"

"I am."

Exultantly he carried her through the house and up the stairs to his bedroom...

Outside the storm continued to rage unabated, but neither Jude nor Cate noticed. Their limbs coiled, hands clasped, their mouths passionately locked, they were sealed off in another landscape. One so extravagantly beautiful and full of sensation they never wanted to leave.

Sunlight lay on the polished floor and on the rug, highlighting the vibrant colours in the design. The sea breeze played with the unlined cream curtains at the French doors. He lifted himself onto an elbow staring down at her. He thought he had never seen anything lovelier in his life. Long dark russet eyelashes lay against her cheeks. Her lips were faintly parted, her breath quiet. The sheet had fallen back to reveal one creamy rounded breast. Very slowly he traced the dusky pink aureole around a nipple with one finger, moving ever closer to the sensitive bud.

Sex with Cate was the kind of sex that had never happened to him. He'd thought he'd had good sex, even great sex at times, but what had happened last night he didn't know he could find a word for. Rapture? Ecstasy, agony? Complete loss of self? He still had the delirium of passion in his blood.

Her beautiful body stirred beneath his hand. Her nipple

thickened and hardened. He bent his head over her, kissed it then her mouth. Deeply.

"Good morning," he murmured, when he finally raised his head. "Are you all right?"

She looked up at him, green eyes wide. "All right?" she asked in a kind of wonderment. "Yes, yes, yes! I've never felt better in my life." She pulled his face down to her. "I think I might stay here forever."

"That's good," he said very softly, "because I don't think I can bear to lct you go. You're amazing."

"So are you." She moved to accommodate her body to his. "Make love to me, Jude. You're so good at it."

"But then you make it so easy." He stripped the top sheet off them, dropped it to the floor...

Afterwards they showered together, soaping each other all over. It took time. Kissing, caressing...Jude lifted her off her feet to take her again.

"I must go to the gallery," she said much later. "I have work to do even though I can't think of anything else but you."

"I have a meeting, too," he said, thrusting his arm into a blue cotton shirt. "I have to report to dear old Ralph. Keep him happy."

"Oh, Ralph," she groaned. Cate was fully dressed now, brushing out her long copper hair. "I meant what I said, Jude. I don't want anything to do with Lester Rogan's money."

He looked back at her, his eyes moving over her lovingly. "I can understand your feelings, Cate, but don't come to any decision before you know the full story. We're searching through Dad's things when maybe we should be searching through Lester's? He may have a bank box stashed away. I'm sure Ralph has already checked his father's safe.''

''I don't think I could bring myself to see Ralph Rogan again, Jude,'' Cate said. ''I don't know how he's controlling himself when he's completely unpredictable.''

''Leave him to me,'' Jude told her calmly. ''What time do you close the gallery?'' He picked up a brush, ran it over his thick, curly hair.

''Five.'' He looked so blazingly handsome, so wonderfully masculine, Cate thought she should really be wearing sunglasses. After such intimacies, such glorious lovemaking she felt warm and happy inside but she knew only too well life was cruel. In the golden heat she couldn't suppress a shiver. Experience had taught her happiness could be spirited away overnight.

Jude was smiling at her, the dimple flicking in his cheek. ''I'll pick you up.'' He quickened his pace of dressing so he could get her car out for her. He had an intense desire to make life easier for Cate in any way he could.

CHAPTER TEN

WHILE Cate at her gallery was tending to a party of Japanese tourists in search of high quality crystals, Jude was closeted with Ralph in his late father's office.

Jude had shown Ralph the framed photograph of his father and friends on board Calypso some thirty years before. Now Ralph was staring down at it, resting his head in his hands. "This is her father?" he asked for perhaps the fourth time.

"I've already told you, Ralph. It is."

Ralph's dark gaze was sober and direct. "And Jimmy swears this man and Dad acted like friends?"

"More than that, Ralph. Jimmy gained the clear impression they were life-long friends. At the very least they'd known one another for years. Cate's father was Dermot Costello, he migrated from Ireland in the early seventies, I checked it out. I checked out his career as an architect and academic as well. He was killed in a car crash when Cate was ten. Her mother remarried. I didn't find a thing on your father before he arrived in North Queensland."

Ralph shifted his attention from Jude back to the framed photograph. "Dad was a mystery man. You'd swear he didn't have another life before he came here. He didn't talk about himself, his family—even he must have had one—he certainly never said anything about being born in Ireland. This Costello guy looks like some guy in the movies."

"Too damned soft!" Ralph hissed through his strong white teeth. "They couldn't have been related. Look at Dad! Hell, I could be looking at myself."

Jude nodded. "I've been searching through all my father's files and papers," Jude said. "It's a big job, I haven't finished yet, but what about your father's papers? I assume you checked out the contents of his wall safe and that desk?"

Ralph snorted. "I would have checked the safe had I known the combination."

"You don't know it?" Jude asked in amazement.

"You don't really think Dad told me. He was obsessively secretive."

"But he'd have to tell someone? He knew he was dying. Your mother doesn't know?"

"Don't you think I'd have gotten it out of her?" Ralph groaned. "I'm fully prepared to call in a guy who knows how to crack safes."

"You've checked all the drawers of that desk?" Jude asked. "He must have kept the combination close."

"Couldn't have been closer," Ralph said. "In his head."

"Why don't we try something?" Jude raised himself out of his chair staring at a painting on the wall behind which he knew there was a safe.

"You don't really think we could come up with the combination?" Ralph gave a scornful smile.

"It's not unusual for people to use numbers that have some significance. Birth dates, lucky numbers."

"Man, you could search forever," Ralph said.

The search in fact took less than ten minutes. After a number of tries with numbers, Jude turned back to Lester Rogan's massive mahogany desk. He found the combination to the safe, pasted carefully to the underside of a bottom drawer.

"Hell!" Ralph said. "Why didn't I think of that?"

Jude shrugged. "Didn't take much imagination."

Jude unlocked the safe. Ralph reached in.

* * *

Late morning as Cate was answering another tourist's questions about crystals associated with spiritual development, a stunning blonde wearing a chocolate-brown leopard print camisole with a cream lace trim and tight-legged cream pants entered the gallery.

Cate smiled at her. "Won't be a moment. Feel free to browse."

"I will." The blonde proceeded to move around the gallery on four-inch heels humming tunelessly.

A few minutes more and Cate had boxed and gift wrapped a particularly beautiful aquamarine sphere, more green than blue, that emitted a gentle energy when held in the palm. The Asian tourist on a day trip to the mainland from her luxury resort on a Great Barrier Reef island thanked her with a charming bow and left.

Cate approached the young woman with the spectacular figure. She was holding a rainbow obsidian to the light. "Are you looking for anything in particular?" Cate asked pleasantly. "That crystal is supposed to bring gratification and enjoyment to one's life."

The blonde turned her voluptuous body full on to face Cate. "You surely don't believe all that twaddle?"

Cate ignore the rudeness. "Crystals have been revered since the dawn of time," she said in a normal friendly tone. "They've been found in the ancient tombs of Egypt, Babylonia and China. The Mayan, Aztec, Celtic, American Indian and African civilisations used crystals, the treasures of the earth in their ceremonies. Many people believe crystals act as catalysts to assist in all kinds of healing processes. The Asian lady who just left the gallery uses crystals for meditation, others for protection. It's a big area of study."

"Spare me." The blonde put the lustrous chunk of volcanic glass back onto the shelf. "You're Cate Costello, aren't you?" She looked Cate up and down.

"I am." Cate knew immediately her visitor wasn't somebody who would brighten her day.

"Poppy Gooding," the blonde announced, her eyes continuing her close inspection. "Jude's girlfriend," she added by way of explanation. "A little bird tells me you've been spending some time with him?"

Though she was shaken, somehow Cate retained her poise. "What little bird would that be?" she asked, knowing she wasn't going to like this one little bit.

"You sure you want to know?" Poppy raised a pencilled brow. "I hope Jude hasn't been sleeping with you, dear, because his loyalty is very important to me. We're going to be married."

"Of course you are," Cate said in the ironic voice of one who knew all about bitter blows. "You're going to be happy forever and ever."

Her visitor looked shocked by her answer. "What's the big joke?" she demanded, with considerable indignation. "I'm deadly serious. I'm up here in this godforsaken place to tell you to lay off my man."

Cate looked past Poppy Gooding's smooth tanned shoulder to the courtyard. "Why don't you deliver that message to Jude," she suggested. "As a matter of fact you can do it right now. He's just pulled up."

"Wonderful! I've got to see him!" Poppy went rushing to the door, in the process losing one of her backless sandals. "Jude!" she screeched out the door, a sound that assaulted more than charmed the ears.

How's that for a greeting, Cate thought. She swiftly positioned herself behind the counter. She might as well look out. Poppy was surging towards Jude like a crocodile surging through a tropical lagoon. It was a wonder she wasn't shedding her clothes while she was at it, Cate thought bitterly. What do I really know about him? Cate, so new to happiness, was starting the familiar slide into bleakness. Had she forgotten men were born liars?

Poppy didn't bother to control her desire even though there were lots of people about. She flung her arms around Jude, kissing him so passionately Cate thought it would take time for Jude's lips to heal. Afterwards Poppy threw back her blond head in an excess of joy at their reunion.

"What a fool I am!" Cate moaned quietly to herself. She had come to understand resignation. But surely a man couldn't commit to a woman the way Jude had committed to her that very morning and have plans to marry the boss's daughter? A woman who looked so damned happy to see him.

Why not? Men couldn't control their sexual urges.

Go away, the both of you! She had to escape again. Go someplace else. She thought of New Zealand. That wasn't far enough. Fiji? She dredged up Jude's remark about Poppy Gooding being irrelevant. She was tempted to go out and tell him what she thought of him, but she had too much pride.

Jude! she mourned. Only this morning he'd been the answer to her prayers. The man she'd been born for. As for the fortune Lester Rogan had left her? They could give it to a retirement home for cats.

Cate left her post at the window, hurriedly picking up the Closed sign and hanging it on the glass door. She couldn't leave because she would have to go past them to get to her car, but she could lock herself in her bedroom and shut the blind. When they'd gone she could come out again and open up shop.

Why? At that point she really didn't know what she was

going to do. She thought she'd been through enough, but it seemed the pain of loss was her dismal lot.

Outside in the courtyard Jude had seen the Closed sign go up on the door. He caught sight of Cate's face. The freeze hit him like a blast. Of course he would change that as soon as he could but first he had to deal with Poppy. He'd always known one day Poppy would present a problem.

"What did you say to Cate?" he asked, not at all nicely.

But Poppy laughed gaily. "I told her I was the girl you were going to marry. You are going to marry me, aren't you, Jude, darling?"

"Don't be so ridiculous," Jude said. "Isn't it time you realised you can't get everything you want, Poppy? Like my head on a plate? Marriage is a very serious business, not a hunt."

"So?" Poppy opened her dark eyes wide. "Don't you think I'm taking you seriously enough, darling? I've travelled all the way up here—actually I'm staying on Hayman I want you to come over—just to be with you."

"Who told you I was here?" Jude asked tersely.

"Jude, darling, it's easy to find out anything if you really want to. I even found out about your redhead. I forgive you. I suppose you were bored."

"I'm madly, deeply, irrevocably in love with her," Jude said. His blue eyes were so fierce they looked like they were capable of starting a fire.

"Love her," Poppy shrieked, throwing her full lung power behind it. "She's ugly. She's got no bust. I hate her hair. I bet it comes out of a bottle."

"I wouldn't care if it did. Yours looks great. But no, Cate's colour is natural. She's beautiful, Poppy. Perfect You've deluded yourself into thinking you're in love with me. You're not. You don't even know me."

"Of course I do," Poppy fumed, moving her body right up close to Jude's. "You've led me on, Jude. You know you have. You let me know what you had in store for me and dad approved of you. Do you know what that could mean? What do you suppose he'll say when I tell him you've thrown me over?"

"Why don't you tell him the truth, Poppy? You decided it was only infatuation. You're over it."

Poppy lifted her head with the greatest disdain. "You're not going to get off the hook as easily as that, Jude. No—one—dumps—me." She reached out to smack a hand into his chest with every word.

"I know a couple of guys who did. Do your worst, Poppy," Jude invited, turning away from her. "I'm thinking of leaving the firm anyway."

"Without references," Poppy yelled after him, the expression on her face too vindictive to ignore.

Jude paused. "That might lead to complications for you, Poppy. You have quite a reputation. Let's face it I could bring charges for sexual harassment in the workplace."

In front of his very eyes, Poppy ground her jaw just like her father. "What did you say?" She stood feet apart, hands on her hips.

"You heard me. Think about it. Go for help. Frankly I think your best chance is to say you dumped me."

Jude knocked at the rear door of the gallery. "You must let me in, Cate," he called, urgency in his voice.

She didn't answer.

He rang her on his mobile, got the answering service. "Love is supposed to be trust, Cate," he said after the beep.

She was having none of that. He rang again with another message. "Poppy Gooding is not and never has been part of my love life. She's nothing more than a spoilt brat who's going to get me the sack.''

He prayed she'd respond to that. She didn't. She was going to ignore him when he had vital news to impart. He rang again with another message. ''I'd push an important document I have with me regarding your father under the door only I'm worried I'll set off the alarm. Please, Cate, don't go into remission.''

It only took her a minute to rush from the bedroom where she'd been sprawled on the bed with the back of her hand over her eyes. She came to the door, unlocking it and throwing it back. ''How dare you say that!'' Her green eyes held flames. ''The only sick person around here is you. She came into the gallery looking like a rock star. Did you see how tight her clothes were and those heels! She told me you were going to marry her.''

''And you fell for it?'' Jude groaned. ''Didn't I tell you about this, Cate?''

''You told me she was irrelevant,'' she snapped.

''She is. The man who marries Poppy Gooding for all the luscious body is going to die of boredom.''

She stared back at him with contempt. ''Luscious body? So how long into the relationship did it take for you to find out let alone get bored?''

''Cut it out, Cate,'' he said sternly. He shifted her bodily out of the way, striding into the living area. ''I know you've had a hell of a life but if we're going to stay together you have to trust me.''

''As if any woman would be crazy enough to trust you,'' Cate said in disgust.

''Okay.'' His blue eyes slashed her. ''You don't have to put up with me a minute longer than necessary. You've got big problems, Cate and I don't know whether you're capable of solving them. How do I know sex to you isn't a bit of a game? Why should I trust you with my heart? Bad things have happened to me, too, you know, I still know how to reach out. You apparently don't or won't. This document—'' he threw it down on the coffee table ''—was found in Lester Rogan's safe. In it he confesses to having stolen a very valuable diamond necklace belonging to your father's grandmother, Lady Elizabeth Costello more than thirty years ago. Your father was blamed for it. He was a younger son and in some financial trouble at the time. Nothing too serious, the sort of debts a university student with a rich father runs up.''

As Jude spoke, obviously angry and disillusioned with her, Cate sank into a chair, almost beyond hearing.

Jude continued. ''Rogan is related to you I'm afraid. He's your father's half brother. Illegitimate as they used to say. Your grandfather must have had an eye for a good-looking woman. Rogan's mother lived and worked on a small farm, one of a number, owned by the Costello family who must have been local land owners. Rogan told no one of course. He kept the theft to himself, no doubt he thought your family owed him, to my mind they did. When your father migrated to Australia to all intents and purposes disgraced, Rogan followed. He told no one about the necklace and had it broken up so he could dispose of the stones. Apparently the necklace was a known piece.'' Jude looked up at Cate but her face showed no emotion so he went on, ''He kept in touch with your father up until your father's death. He knew about you and all about your mother's disappearance. He determined towards the end of his life he was going to make it up to you for the terrible injustice he'd done to your father. It's all there, Cate. He goes into a lot more detail than I'm saying. He must have genuinely cared about your father who never looked down on him or denied the relationship like the rest of your family. Your father treated him as a brother.

"I'll go now. Read through it carefully. Come to a decision. Personally I think you're entitled to a good deal, you and your father's memory. Rogan prospered greatly from the sale of the diamonds in that necklace. He wants the full story to be known."

Cate sat for some time after Jude left. A sense of unreality had overtaken her. Every one in her life had treated her like a fool. Every one of them had secrets. If her father had privately acknowledged Lester Rogan as his half brother why hadn't he presented him to his family, her mother and her? Or in turning into a pillar of society had her father rejected the relationship? She would never know. Couldn't Lester Rogan at some point have told her he was related to her? Obviously not. She was the one who had to be kept in the dark. Had Rogan been instrumental in some way in getting her up here? Tony replying to one of her letters had encouraged her to make the move, telling her about the gallery. Had Lester Rogan influenced Tony's offer? Then, on top of everything, she had Poppy Gooding burst in on her claiming she and Jude had enjoyed a relationship close enough to discuss marriage.

Hadn't her trust in the world been shattered when she lost her father? Utterly destroyed with the disappearance of her mother? As she'd thought so many times chaos was everywhere.

Sunk in her sad reflections Cate was slow to hear footsteps coming across the deck. Startled she looked up to see Miss Forsyth holding her hand up to the window, peering in. Miss Forsyth spotted her, waved.

Cate rose from her chair and went to the door.

"I say, m'dear, you don't look happy?" Miss Forsyth

greeted her, grey eyes keen. "Aren't you well? Is that why you closed the gallery?"

"It's a long story, Miss Forsyth," Cate said. "Please come in."

"I'm not disturbing you, Cate?" Miss Forsyth looked her concern. "You seem to be speaking with an effort?"

"I had a falling out with Jude," Cate explained.

"I see," Miss Forsyth nodded sagely, as though she knew exactly what that might mean. "May I ask about what?"

Cate gave an odd little laugh. "You mightn't believe this but his girlfriend pursued him up here."

"You don't mean that silly Poppy person?" Miss Forsyth asked, sounding amazed.

"How do you know about her?" Cate was equally surprised. She waved Miss Forsyth into a chair.

"Jude must have told Jimmy a little bit about her." Miss Forsyth made herself comfortable, rearranging cushions. "Jimmy tells me everything as you know. I think Jude looked on her more as a work hazard than a girlfriend, m'dear. Isn't she his boss's daughter? I'm sure Jimmy told me that. And she chased him up here? Mind you Jude is the sort of young man the girls chase. That smile and the blue eyes! So you were jealous?"

'It's really weird what happens to me." Wearily Cate shook her head. "Do you believe in love at first sight, Miss Forsyth?"

Miss Forsyth smiled. "I'm not going to argue with a man of Will Shakespeare's intelligence and knowledge of human nature. Are you telling me you're in love with Jude?"

Cate nodded. "I was on Cloud Ten this morning, until she arrived."

"And Jude is angry you don't trust him?"

"That's actually not true, I do trust him. The fault lies in me. I'm one of those people in the world who have lost their capacity to trust. I can't believe in happiness, or rather I can't believe in happiness for me. Up to date I feel I was born to lose out.''

"Because you have a sad story to tell. Wounds to heal. I've felt it all along. I've said to Jimmy many a time, there's a girl who has suffered. Why don't you tell me all about it, m'dear,'' Miss Forsyth urged, her expression wonderfully kind. "It does no good to keep so much in. I believe we're put on this earth to help each other and I desperately want to help you.''

"You're such a kind woman, Miss Forsyth. You and Jimmy have been very supportive right from the beginning. You deserve to know.'' Cate met the older woman's eyes. "I only wish what I have to say weren't so terrible but I have the feeling you'll take it all in your stride. You're a strong woman, a good friend.''

Cate leaned forward, picking up the document Jude had left her. She remembered the sternness of his expression. She'd thought before today one didn't trifle with a man like Jude Conroy.

"I have a letter from Lester Rogan right here, Miss Forsyth. Written in his own hand. It's a confession to a crime of theft he committed over thirty years ago, but first I want to tell you about my life before I came here. I'm sorry I haven't done so before, but it was so traumatic. I'm still trying to cope. Anyway, you deserve to know.''

CHAPTER ELEVEN

"SO WE'VE got a situation here," Ralph Rogan summed up an hour-long family discussion at the dinner table. He regarded his mother and sister with brooding dark eyes. "We've got to sort it out.

"She's our kin." Melinda shook her head from side to side, still in a state of shock. "How could Dad have kept that from us? He's known about her existence for over twenty years. Her father was Dad's half brother. I don't believe it. That makes her our what?"

"Your cousin, dear," Myra said, shuffling her knife and fork. "Your father was a very strange man, but I believe what he did haunted him for the rest of his days. It was bad."

"He must have been desperate," Ralph said. "Those people, the Costellos must have had everything. Dad had nothing. He must have watched them up at the big house while he and his mother probably lived in poverty or near enough, the lot of them looking down their fine patrician noses."

"That doesn't excuse what he did, Ralph," Melinda reasoned, her eyes and eyelids, pink from crying.

"Especially when he left someone else take the blame," Ralph added harshly. "I wonder if her father ever suspected Dad was the one?"

"Who knows!" Myra shrugged. "He must have had his suspicions. Must have. Lester always had a dark side to him. Even then. He never loved me, he married me because he considered it a smart business move. It was a takeover. His bankroll was no more than ill-gotten gains."

"He stole so he could have a future," Ralph frowned at his mother darkly. "He was just trying to survive."

"Don't condone it, Ralph," Melinda pleaded. "What must she think of us?"

"Who cares what she thinks of us," Ralph growled. "No matter what Dad did then, he made his own fortune since. That fortune should have been left to us not her. She's not going to have it."

"Perhaps she's entitled to it," Myra said. "Or a lot of it. It's horrible her mother disappearing like that. People simply don't vanish off the face of the earth."

"Some do," Ralph grunted, obviously not interested. "She might have wanted to get away. She might have committed suicide. Who knows? It doesn't matter to us."

"She's our cousin, Ralph," Melinda pointed out, a catch in her voice.

"You want a cousin?" Ralph glared at her, venting his turbulent frustrations. "This is bloody hard to take. All right—" he threw up a hand "—maybe she's entitled to something, but not what Dad left her. I swear, we're going to hang on to that. The way Dad treated us! Then the old hypocrite up and leaves her a fortune. He must have felt he was buying his way into heaven."

"So what time does Jude want us all to meet?" Myra asked fatalistically.

"Ten in the morning." An odd smile played around his mouth. "You know he's sweet on her," he said, staring at his sister.

"How can he be?" Melinda blinked. "He barely knows her."

"Sorry to disappoint you, sis." Ralph lifted his beer glass and drained off the contents. "It was obvious. You've seen her and you've seen yourself in the mirror. Why would he look at you?"

Myra drew a long breath. "You know, Ralph, you're genuinely cruel. You take after your father I'm afraid. I've had so much unhappiness in my life and I simply bowed under it instead of putting up a fight. I let your father get away with all his crimes and misdemeanours. I've allowed you to treat me and your sister with contempt, when neither of us deserve it. That's over. You must leave this house."

"You're turning on me, too?" Passion blazed in Ralph's face.

"To tell you the truth, Ralph, I no longer care about you," Myra replied quietly. "You've killed all my love. You'll be better away from us anyway. Your father didn't leave any of us penniless. You've got plenty."

Ralph stood up yanking his chair back from the table. "Don't think I'm going to let things stand," he said in a hard, jarring voice. "So she's family, of sorts. I'll hire the best lawyers in the country to make her hand most of it back."

"Go to litigation and you could lose everything," Melinda reminded him, then added in a clear mocking tone. "Why don't you marry that old sexpot Amy Gibson? Make an honest woman out of her. You've been using her for years."

"Whereas you're missing out on sex wholesale," Ralph gave a humourless laugh. "No one going to marry you, Mel. You're a born old maid."

"Don't be so sure," Melinda called as her brother left the room. "Mum and I have lots of plans for after you're gone."

Jude arrived at the gallery around nine-thirty for the ten o'clock appointment at the Rogan mansion. That allowed him a few moments to speak to Cate privately before they made the drive. He'd spoken to Cate briefly by phone the previous evening regarding the meeting he'd set up with the family. He half expected her to decline, she sounded played out. For that matter he was far from on top of the world. Her lack of trust in him had hit him where it hurt. There was also the stunning fact somewhere around midnight as he sought to get Cate out of his mind by prowling the house, he'd uncovered another secret he dearly wished had been left untold. He'd found hidden in an old trunk in the attic, one he thought had only contained his favourite childhood books, a bundle of letters his mother had written him from her new home in Connecticut.

Would he ever get over the shock? Would he ever clear his father's duplicity from his mind? He'd read one at random, couldn't bear to read more. Not then. Maybe not ever. The letters began some months after she went away; stopped after several years. His father had never told him.

Why? Why had his father kept his mother's letters from him? Had his father feared he might have wanted to join his mother in America? Had his father feared being left totally alone? Like Cate, Jude was reeling under the impact of so many disclosures.

She greeted him quietly. She was dressed more formally than he had yet seen her in a beautiful lime silk dress with a purple silk border. She had pretty lime coloured high heeled sandals on her feet. Her beautiful hair was pulled back from her face and arranged in an elegant knot at her nape. She wore earrings. He had never seen earrings on her before.

She looked exquisite. Boundlessly beyond him.

"I take it you've given careful consideration to everything Lester Rogan had to say in his letter?" he asked her, sounding far more a lawyer than a lover.

"Of course." She inclined her head. "I showed it to Miss

Forsyth. She arrived yesterday after you'd gone. We dis-cussed it for quite some time.''

''As have the Rogan family. I spoke to Mrs Rogan briefly this morning. She and Myra want very much to meet you. They're nice people, Cate. For all Rogan's money they haven't had an easy life. You need have no worries there.''

''The Rogan family is the least of my worries, thank you Jude. I can't think Ralph is looking forward to seeing me again?''

He let that pass. ''Mrs Rogan has asked him to leave the family home, something she's never had the courage to ask of him before. The women will be much happier without him.''

She turned to meet his eyes. ''I meant what I said about not wanting the money, Jude.''

He shrugged. ''It won't help to give it all back to Ralph. If you really don't want it, there are plenty of very worthy charities. But Lester Rogan wanted absolution, Cate. He wanted forgiveness.''

''He should have looked for it at home. I suppose there is the question of compensation for my father's family. The necklace was probably very valuable. I can't imagine it's worth today.''

Jude stared at her lovely withdrawn face. ''Let's get this meeting over first and see what they all have to say. I advise against any immediate decisions. You're in a highly emo-tional state. You've had to withstand shock after shock.''

She bit her lip. ''I'm sorry about yesterday.''

''So am I,'' he said briefly. ''Shall we go?''

Myra looking better than she had in a long while greeted them at the door. Her gentle eyes took only a few seconds to weigh up the lovely young woman who stood so composedly beside Jude. A wave of emotion passed across Myra's face. She reached for Cate's hand.

"Welcome, my dear," she said warmly. That broke the ice. Spontaneously, both women leaned forward to brush cheeks. "Good morning, Jude." Myra's emotion filled eyes moved on to him. "Please come in, both of you. We're in the living room."

Melinda sprang up from her armchair immediately they walked in, a smile that echoed her mother's on her small, pretty face. After a moment Ralph dragged himself up.

Jude prayed for a miracle. Most of all he prayed he could find a way to make Cate really love him. She might have dinted his pride but pride couldn't be allowed to stand in the way of love.

There was a long silence as they drove home in the car. Both of them felt they had talked themselves out. Cate made no objection when Jude suggested briefly they could go back to his place rather than the gallery.

Good, he thought. You trust me.

They were barely inside the door when he drew her to him, holding her lightly not wanting to make her the least bit nervous. "You did wonderfully back there, Cate," he said. "I can't imagine anyone doing it better and in such a difficult situation. You've made quite a number of concessions but I guess they're yours to make. The family seems happy. Even Ralph."

"I'm not interested in the real estate business anyway," Cate said, moving gently out of his arms. "You were right about Myra and Melinda. They're sweet. I never expected they would accept me so readily."

"Why not?" Jude shrugged, following her into the living room. "They're prepared to care about you, Cate. You took the wind out of Ralph's sails in a matter of minutes. He thought he was going to have a big fight on his hands.''

"I just wanted to be fair, Jude.''

"I know.'' Jude felt the tension build up in his chest. It was all or nothing now. Love or heartbreak.

"When I feel calmer about all this I'll clear my father's name,'' Cate was saying, her head bent in a pose of contemplation. "I'll also compensate his family for their loss of the necklace.''

"Your family, Cate,'' he pointed out quietly.

"Maybe.'' There was a sad curve to her lips. "But they let my father go out of their lives. I can't forgive them for that. They didn't care if he had a family here in Australia. They wouldn't care about me.''

"What do any of us know?'' Jude asked, broodingly. "I was so sure my mother totally abandoned me, but I was wrong. I had a momentous find last night. I've been waiting for the right moment to tell you.''

She turned about, smiled at him. Not a full smile. More like she was pained or holding something back. "What is it?''

It took all his willpower not to go to her and pull her into his arms. Kiss her over and over. Her mouth, her neck, her eyes, her cheeks. But nothing against her wishes. "A bundle of letters,'' he said, his voice vibrating with emotion. "I don't think I would have found then only I couldn't settle after our senseless argument. It left me quite shattered. Poppy Gooding means absolutely nothing to me, Cate,'' he insisted, his blue gaze searing. "I thought you should have known that. I thought you'd realize I couldn't possibly make love to a woman like I've made love to you and be involved with someone else.''

Colour burned in her cheeks. She moved closer with no

hesitation. "I'm sorry, Jude. I have trouble believing in happiness."

"You doubt I'm madly in love you?" His voice held a tormented note.

"It's all the baggage I carry, Jude. Forgive me." Her beautiful green eyes focused on him with intensity. "Tell me about the letters. Who were they from?"

He made a bewildered gesture with his head. "They were from my mother to me."

There was such a haunted look in his eyes Cate felt her own eyes sting. "How extraordinary!" she said, a faint tremor running through her body. "And your father didn't ever show them to you?"

"No." Jude's voice revealed his sense of betrayal. "I lived with him all my life. I loved him, trusted him, yet he kept my mother's letters from me. I could only read one last night—I was so shocked, mostly with Dad—but I intend to read the lot today. I have to make some tough decisions now. My mother wanted me to come to her."

"I'm sure she did," Cate answered softly, "but you can understand your father's reason for not showing the letters to you? He was terrified he might lose you. He would have been devastated twice over." Cate moved the few remaining steps towards him, her eyes reflecting her depth of feeling.

"I wouldn't have left him," Jude maintained. "I know what happened to him when Mum left, the grief he suffered. But I would have contacted my mother. I would have written. I could have seen her some time. Oh, Cate, I loved her. You don't know how much. She hurt us both dreadfully, but I wish I'd known about the letters."

"Of course you do." Cate studied his handsome, anguished face. The vulnerability of his expression tore at her heart. "But you can still do something, Jude. Most likely your mother lives in the same place and even if she doesn't you could trace her, explain why you never got her letters. Your mother didn't go missing like mine.''

Jude looked up, saw Cate's pain. ''I'm so sorry, Cate. One day something will come to light, you'll see. The police never really close the books on these cases. They'd have their suspicions regarding your stepfather, but obviously they weren't able to charge him with anything. You never did tell them your stepfather's interest in you had disturbing sexual overtones. You should. I'll go with you. Your stepfather if he was involved in your mother's disappearance will make a fatal error one day,'' Jude predicted. As he said it, he believed in his heart that would happen.

''She's not alive.'' Cate dipped her head. ''I have to accept that. But your mother is. You can find her, Jude. You have to make peace with your mother before you can move on.''

He gave a twisted smile. ''We could really build a case for some heavenly intervention here, so many strange things happening to shed light on what really went on in the past.''

This time her smile didn't flicker and disappear. It blossomed. So beautiful it made him think of springtime, flowers, a time of renewal.

''Have you thought it may be the spirit of our parents sending us these messages, Jude?'' she asked, a shining light in her eyes.

He put out a tender hand to stroke her cheek. ''It seems to me, Cate, that's not impossible. You have to admit it's all very strange. Oh, come here to me!'' he groaned, hauling her to him as though he couldn't remain another moment away from the exquisite comfort of her body.

A soft cry issued from Cate's lips. It sounded like pure bliss.

''I've come to realise I'll have nothing if I don't have you,'' Jude muttered, burying his face against her creamy throat, catching the scent off her skin. "I love you in that dress. I hope it's easy to get off." He moved to kiss her with yearning, as if it were his salvation.

"I'm sure you'll find a way," Cate whispered. "If you can't, I'll help."

His laugh was exultant. "No need. I've figured it out already." He gazed into her beautiful eyes, his expression turning serious. "Being with you I feel whole again, Cate. I haven't felt that in a very long time. I don't want us to fight about anything. It's a terrible thing to fight, especially about things that aren't important."

"Then let's start again," she suggested sweetly, her expression very tender and soft.

Love for her burned in him. He smoothed her hair, revelling in the length and its silken feel. "Why start again, when I loved you at first sight? I can't let you go, Cate. I want us to be everything to each other. I never thought I could say this, but I've come to believe we have one true soul mate in life. I'm overwhelmed that I've found her. Now that I have, I want her to marry me. Will you, Cate?"

She felt as though a dazzling light was all around her. A miraculous sensation not easy to dismiss. "You know I will," she said.

"My love!" He bent to kiss her deeply, powerfully, as though he meant to reach her soul. "I want us to face life together," he told her after he lifted his head. "Wherever we decide that might be. I'll be saying goodbye to Gooding, Carter & Legge but there are other firms. I might even start up my own. There's plenty going on in the North these days and I don't ever want to part with this house."

"Oh, no, I love it!" Cate said with fervour. She had loved it from the beginning, its flowing warmth, its serenity, the streaming golden light.

"So do I. And it's welcomed you." He held her beloved

body fast." You've even seen our resident ghost. It's supposed to appear to people at a crossroad in their life, you know, so the legend goes. I want us to be full partners, Cate. I want us to take on all the joys, all the risks. Anything, as long as we face it together."

She leaned back in his arms, green eyes luminous, her expression divinely happy. "Marry me must be among the loveliest words in the language." ·

"You've made me believe that, too." It was true. The love he thought stolen from him was like a power within him. "Life would be pretty empty without a soul mate. Fate drew us together, Cate. It wasn't chance."

"No." Cate had to whisper her agreement her heart was so full. "We need one another, Jude, to be complete."

It was a message Jude welcomed with all his heart. "Do you want me to carry you upstairs?" His blue eyes as he looked down on her were ablaze with desire.

"I'd like nothing better," Cate sweetly said, her silky arms sliding up to tenderly encircle his neck.

A new life was opening up before her and it filled her with wonder.

Harlequin Romance®

presents
an exciting new duet by
international bestselling author
Lucy Gordon

Where there's a will, there's a wedding!

Rinaldo and Gino Farnese are wealthy, proud, passionate brothers who live in the heart of Tuscany, Italy. Their late father's will brings one surprise that ultimately leads to two more— a bride for each of them!

Don't miss book 2:

Gino's Arranged Bride, #3807

On-sale August!

Available wherever Harlequin books are sold.

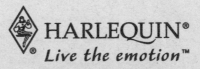

The world's bestselling romance series.

HARLEQUIN® Presents

Seduction and Passion Guaranteed!

We are pleased to announce
Sandra Marton's fantastic new series

The O'CONNELLS

In order to marry, they've got to gamble on love!

Don't miss...

KEIR O'CONNELL'S MISTRESS

Keir O'Connell knew it was time to leave Las Vegas when he became consumed with desire for a dancer. The heat of the desert must have addled his brain! He headed east and set himself up in business— but thoughts of the dancing girl wouldn't leave his head. And then one day there she was, Cassie...

Harlequin Presents #2309
On sale March 2003

Pick up a Harlequin Presents® novel and you will enter a world of spine-tingling passion and provocative, tantalizing romance!

Available wherever Harlequin books are sold.

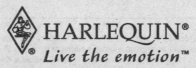

HARLEQUIN®
Live the emotion™

Visit us at www.eHarlequin.com

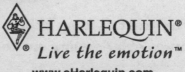